SO EASY

By Lynn M. Miller

"Trust yourself. Create the kind of self that you will be happy to live with all your life."

Golda Meir

This book is dedicated

to everyone who said, "Write another one!"

You know who you are and I love you for it!

This is a complete work of fiction. Any reference to anyone living or dead is purely unintentional. Although ***SO EASY*** *is technically a sequel to the novel* ***IN JEOPARDY!*** *it can be read independently.*

ISBN: 978-0-9842249-3-7
Spitz Press LLC

TABLE OF CONTENTS:

CHAPTER ONE

September, 2004

Jen dropped the bomb when she and Sara were working on dinner together. She was brushing olive oil on a whole chicken while Sara was slicing cooked redskins for potato salad. “I don’t think I want to be an investment advisor, Aunt Sara,” she said. I know you’ve given me this great opportunity to apprentice in your office, but I don’t think it’s for me. Jen didn’t look up and she wasn’t smiling, which was unusual. If Sara had to guess, she would even say that Jen looked frightened about bringing the subject up.

Sara looked over at her niece, surprised. *Why ever would she be afraid to tell me anything?* she thought. She knew better than to voice that, so she calmly replied, “Well that’s OK. You certainly don’t have to do anything you don’t want to do.” She hesitated, continuing to slice methodically, and then went on. “I’m surprised though. I thought you loved working in the office. I always see you laughing at Jimmy Frank and I thought you genuinely enjoyed researching investments and matching them with clients. You’ve done so well at everything. Why would you say this?”

Just then, as if on cue, Jen's phone went off. She looked relieved. "Let me just get that, OK?" Jen grabbed her cell phone and rushed outside to take the call. Sara frowned. It wasn't normal for Jen not to take a call in front of her. Something was up. She added chopped celery, red bell pepper and onion to the potatoes, squirted on Dijon mustard and mayonnaise and seasoned the salad with salt and pepper. She took a quick taste and added a bit more pepper. As she was putting it in the fridge to chill, Jen returned and started sprinkling salt, pepper and cayenne on the chicken.

Sara looked over at her niece who seemed unusually aloof. Clearly there was something she was hiding. She hoped there was nothing seriously wrong. She couldn't help but admire Jen. She was such a pretty girl. Her thick, curly hair was pulled back in a high ponytail and still reached her waist. Jen was witty, sweet and popular – all rolled into a beautiful package that made boys flock after her. Jen was definitely not the boy crazy type though and clearly found them annoying. Sara shrugged off her feeling of malaise. That was probably it – an issue with a boy and that was all. Nothing to worry about.

Then suddenly Jen was talking hurriedly. "Aunt Sara, thanks so much for the offer of dinner but I have to run. The oven is hot now. You said 400 degrees, right? So I'll just pop this chicken in there and you and Uncle Peter can eat in an hour. I'll stay to eat another time." The roaster pan of chicken went into the oven. They blew kisses to each other and Jen made her exit so fast that Sara hardly had time to speak. *I wonder what that was all about,* she thought. *I'll have to try and pin her down for more information tomorrow at the office.*

When the door closed behind Jen, she signed with relief. The call had been from Greg Smythe, the newest investment advisor in the office. He was a lot older than she was and her aunt would go ballistic if she knew. Things were getting serious and she was having trouble hiding it at the office too – let alone from her aunt who could see right through her. At least it had always seemed that way. They had always been close but Jen always felt like a glass mirror when Sara was around. She wasn't sure what she was going to do about it because she needed more time. It wasn't at all what she was sure everyone was thinking. Not at all. Jen quickly got in her car and peeled out of the driveway.

Unfortunately hearing the car take off like that fueled Sara's suspicions. She could hardly wait for the next day in the office when she could approach her niece and have a real discussion.

Sara was still thinking about what could possibly be wrong with Jen when Peter showed up. He was an hour later than the time they had agreed on for dinner. By then, she had set the table in the kitchen and steamed some broccoli, seasoning it with butter, salt and pepper. It had been turned down to simmer for quite a while and was getting a little mushy. She was just opening a bottle of Turley Zinfandel when he came through the door, pecked her on the cheek and went into his office to drop his briefcase. She thought she smelled liquor on his breath. *Is that why he was late?* she wondered. *Did he stop at the bar on his way home again?* Instantly in a foul mood, she pulled the chicken out of the oven which had also long been turned down and the potato salad from the fridge, setting them on the table for dinner.

When her husband came back, he seemed preoccupied and not in the best mood. So Sara decided not to bother him about her concerns about Jen or the fact that he was late. She knew he adored her beautiful niece and it would greatly concern him. Instead, she flipped on the news on the big screen television on the wall behind the kitchen table. They sat down together in front of it to eat. There was a bit of small talk, but for the most part they ate in silence. When she started picking up the dishes, he said he needed to catch up on some paperwork and retired to his office.

She frowned. *That was fulfilling,* she thought sarcastically.

Sara put the dishes in the dishwasher slowly. She felt disassociated with her husband, and hurt. *How many evenings had been so similar to this? Why was conversation so non-existent or stilted? Why couldn't she think of much to say to him? Why didn't he say much to her? Did she even know him anymore?*

She longed for the old days when they were inseparable best friends. She remembered the first time she saw him – a tall, lanky, handsome man across a crowded room. It was at the wedding reception of her best friend. She had been the Maid of Honor and was wearing a ridiculous purple dress chosen by the bride. It didn't suit her at all, but he noticed her looking at him and his easy smile had made her heart flutter. It was love at first sight on both sides. He had immediately crossed the room to introduce himself and to offer her a drink. *The rest is history,* she thought.

Maybe it was all her? Maybe she had driven him away? She resolved to be a better wife, to communicate more and to plan fun evenings like she had long ago. She knew she loved him and she knew she could make things better. Life had just taken them in different directions. She knew she could fix it.

Peter wasn't having the best day either. He sat at his desk, ignoring the work he had used for an excuse to get away. Instead, he was thinking about his relationship with Sara. He was sick of her late nights and late mornings. It meant he hardly ever saw her. Dinner being ready at home was a rarity. He hadn't expected her to follow through on it tonight either. That's why he had stopped at the bar – to pass the time and to talk with people who cared about him. Plus a few drinks made him relax and feel so much better.

He was also sick of all of her worries over her clients – sick of hearing about it. It's all she thought about. *There was never any time for him anymore. What about his worries and problems?* He thought about the account he had started that she didn't know about. She had no idea how much money he really made and it had been easy to keep it from her.

So it had come to this. Secrets and lies. He wondered if there were any on her part. *Probably,* he thought pessimistically. He was sure she was as unhappy as he was. She had hardly spoken to him at dinner. Suddenly it occurred to him that it would be so easy just to walk away. So easy. There were no children to think about. Unfortunately. He had really wanted children, but understood when she said that she was unable to conceive. At least that's what she had said. Maybe she simply didn't want any. Maybe that was it. Could he really be sure?

She had certainly made a case for not adopting a child. He had listened to her reasons, but what they all boiled down to in his mind was that she didn't want to interrupt her career. At first it was all right, but in the long run, not being a father bugged him a lot more than he had expected.

Peter sighed and got out the papers he needed to review. He sat up late and when he went to bed Sara was already asleep. *Par for the course,* he thought. He felt like he was living alone.

CHAPTER TWO

When Sara woke the next morning, Peter was already gone. She rolled over and looked at the clock. *Why hadn't she set an alarm?* She knew one part of the change in her relationship with her husband was that they didn't see each other as much. *Dang. I have to get up earlier. I know it would help.* She resolved to do just that, jumped up and got ready to go to the office as quickly as she could.

When Sara walked into Jordon and Associates Investments that morning, the first thing she saw was Jen coming out of Greg Smythe's office. That in itself was not unusual, but the fact that Jen's face was all red and that she seemed pretty flustered was highly unusual. Greg was a new investment advisor. He had only been there a couple of months, so Sara didn't know him well. On the surface he seemed great and she knew that her Assistant Patsy liked him a lot But she still couldn't help wondering if this had anything to do with Jen's revelation the night before.

Greg was clearly handsome and articulate, despite the fact that his eyes were set very close together and his clothing often looked rumpled. She had grown up with her mother always saying not to trust anyone whose eyes were like that. Despite the fact that she knew it was an old wives' tale, it always gave her an unsettling feeling that had stuck with her.

Greg was also respected for his success and gentlemanly elegance. Despite that, though, he could be very demanding and arrogant, making people feel small. She had heard it from others. Jen wouldn't be the only one if that were the case. There were a lot of people in the hall, so Sara filed the thought away and didn't go after Jen. After all, Jen was there in a professional role and she had to be careful to deal with her as a normal employee.

As Sara was entering her own office, she looked back down the hall and saw Patsy enter Greg's office and slam the door. She frowned. *Now what was that all about?* It was highly unlike Patsy to do something like that. Normally she was very even keeled and cheerful. Obviously something had set her off. *Could it possibly be about Greg and her Jen?* That was hard to believe. He must be fifteen years older than Jen and knew she was Sara's niece. *God forbid,* she thought. *I had better keep an eye on this situation.*

The morning passed quickly with client calls and paperwork. It was lunchtime before Patsy showed up with her mail and a couple of messages she had taken while Sara was on the phone. She was smiling and seemed her usual self.

"Hi, Patsy! Good to see you. Sorry that this morning was so hectic. Have a seat." she said.

Patsy sat down and handed her the papers. "Do you want to go through them?" she asked.

"Not necessary. I'm sure they're very clear and well done as usual." Sara smiled.

"Patsy, is everything OK? I couldn't help but notice you slamming Greg's door this morning and I couldn't help but wonder..." She let her voice trail off without finishing the sentence.

Patsy looked stricken. "Sure. Sure. Everything's OK. Really. Sure."

Sara frowned. "Seriously? That wasn't like you at all."

"I know. But really. Everything's fine. Don't worry about it, OK?" she said brusquely.

"OK, but you know you can talk to me about anything if you need to. I'm always here for you."

"Thanks. I do know that." Patsy started to get up but then sat right back down. "All right. Here goes. There IS something you need to know."

"Look, Sara. It's Jen. I'm convinced she has been stealing from petty cash."

"What?" Sara was incredulous. "Jen has plenty of money and a good job. There would be no reason for her to do that. Are you sure?" she asked.

"I'm sorry, but yes," Patsy countered. "It has disappeared several times when she was the only one who had been around my office. I hate to say it, but I believe it's true. I mean, I know it's true. It couldn't be anyone else."

"Well, could we please keep this to ourselves until I've at least had a chance to talk to Jen about it?"

"Sure," Patsy said. "You do that. Let me know what you find out. She got up to leave, talking as she left the room. "And by the way, the other interns are not happy. They feel like Jen is getting special treatment."

"Susan and Laura? They're Jen's best friends! What kind of special treatment are you talking about?" Her phone rang so she couldn't ask any more questions. Troubled, she answered it and Patsy took the opportunity to duck out of her office. Then before she knew it, the end of the day had arrived and all the girls were gone. She tried to call Jen, but her niece did not pick up. She texted Jen asking for a call back and gathered her things to leave.

As she was leaving, Sara saw Patsy leaving Greg's office again and head for the exit. Patsy looked troubled and angry. *What was going on here?* Before she could act, Greg rushed out of his office with his briefcase and followed her out, so she kept her distance.

Looking at her watch, Sara realized it was 8 pm and she had worked through the dinner hour again. She tried to call Peter but got no answer. Quickly heading home, she ate dinner by herself and went to bed, her thoughts reeling about what could possibly be going on with Jen, Patsy and Greg. *Hopefully I'm exaggerating all of this,* she thought.

She took a sleeping pill – reserved for special occasions when she just couldn't sleep but needed to. She woke late again the next morning, groggy from the pill and slow to get out of bed. Peter had obviously been there and gone. She sighed. She could call him, but all she wanted to do was to fall back to sleep for one more hour. As she dozed off, she made a decision. She would talk to him tomorrow and start making it all up to him. There was plenty of time. They still had a long life to live together. There was no reason it would not all work out.

CHAPTER THREE

Peter had gotten home late and then left early to take care of some loose ends and to prepare for a 1:00 lunch appointment with an important client. He worked right up until he had to leave, then gathered his paperwork, slid it into his briefcase and left quickly. He was on the steps of his office building when he patted his pockets and realized he had left his wallet on his desk after using a credit card to order some printer cartridges on the Internet for their home printer. He didn't have his phone either, so he swore and turned around to go back to the office. *Damn. Now he would be late.* He was halfway back up the steps when it happened. He heard a loud explosion and had a strange sensation of flying just before his world turned black.

Sara and Jake Jordon, her boss and the owner of the firm she worked for, had decided to go for an early lunch together to discuss some office management issues. Although she was not the official Office Manager, he often turned to her for advice because she had been there so long and had played several different office roles. She also intended to ask him if he had any idea what was going on with the interns and with Greg and Patsy. However, she never got the chance.

The restaurant was a local hangout and almost completely full of men in business suits and women in high heels and dresses. She sighed when they tried to get a table only to discover there weren't any. Unfortunately, it wasn't really surprising. The place was a great one for a quick plate of hot food and a drink. They took seats at the bar and ordered sandwiches. They were eating them and having a chat about a better office supply inventory method that would make people more accountable when **BREAKING NEWS** flashed on the television above them. An excited reporter was standing near Copley Square in Boston, periodically coughing from the smoke swirling around him. The words running along the bottom of the screen were chilling. **BOMBING IN DOWNTOWN BOSTON. TOWNLEY BUILDING BLOWN TO BITS.**

The bartender glanced up and saw it too so he immediately grabbed the remote to turn up the volume. As customers were interrupted by the volume and realized what was on the television, they left their tables and gathered around the bar to stare at the screen. Except for the blaring television, there were no other sounds, as shocked patrons tried to digest what was happening.

On the screen was a reporter standing at a street corner several blocks away from the building. Behind him was a scene of complete chaos.

Crowds of people were intermittently walking fast and running. They were covered with what looked like ash and were also coughing. Some were crying. Others were consoling. Still others were screaming. Everyone looked terrified.

The reporter went on excitedly… "To recap… As you can see, we can't get too close so we are a few blocks away from the disaster. About thirty minutes ago, the Townley building was blown to bits. At this time, we cannot rule out a terror attack. Witnesses say that a large van pulled up and stopped in front of the building. Some say they saw the driver – a large man with a beard who was wearing dark clothing - running away. Before they had time to react, the whole thing went up – or I mean, the whole thing came down. It's thought that perhaps there were also other timed explosions because every floor has tumbled to the ground. The sound was deafening. All ten floors have collapsed!"

Sara dropped her sandwich and her mind went blank. She continued to stare at the screen but could hardly concentrate on the reporter's words… "Some escaped but with massive injuries… The hunt for bodies has already begun… Witnesses describe hearing several sounds of explosions."

Her mind was numb. She looked at Jake and tried to speak but her throat constricted and the words came out as a loud whisper. “THAT’S PETER’S BULDING!”

CHAPTER FOUR

Sara felt faint and Jake grabbed her arm to steady her, just as she started to crumple and slide off her seat. "Oh my God, Sara," was all he could get out. He helped her straighten up and kept hold of her arm to steady her. They both continued to stare at the television screen, straining to look for a glimpse of Peter or anyone else they could recognize from his firm. Jake also knew some of them because they had gotten together socially when he had been married. But because of the dust and the chaos, it was nearly impossible to identify anyone.

Sara stood and blurted out, "I have to go there! It's impossible. It can't be true!"

Jake tried to speak slowly to help her calm down and said, "Look. Look at the bottom of the screen. See the running type? It says to stay away. The police and rescue teams don't want any more congestion. They need to help people get out, get away and to start looking for those trapped in the wreckage. Try to relax. I'm sure he's fine. We don't even know if he was in there. I'm sure he will call you soon."

Tears were now streaming down Sara's face, but she sat down. She put her head on her folded arms and gave in to the sobs. Sirens started to blare in the background, making the scene all too real. To her, the sounds were piercing her brain.

“Get your phone out, Sara” Jake said. “Try and call him. Hopefully he will answer and we’ll know right away.”

“Yes,” she said. “Yes.”

She called… and called… and called again. No answer. Nothing. The phone rang and his voice mail message came on. It was hell hearing his cheerily recorded voice.

“Hi! This is Peter Jensen. Please leave your name and number and I’ll get back to you as soon as I can.” She cringed because she could almost hear him smiling as he recited the message. Every time she listened to it she was overwhelmed with regret for every second of their last few times together. *Why did I wait to make things right? Why was I such a horrible wife? Why was I so out of tune with him? Why? Why? Why?*

Jake calmly and firmly said, “Sara, double check and make sure your ringer is turned on.” On auto-pilot, she nodded and flipped the lever on the side of her phone. He was right. She had left it off after her last meeting earlier in the day.

Somehow that was reassuring – to at least know that Peter could reach her when he tried. But the news continued and it was not good. They started to show survivors on the air so their families would know they were OK, stopping them and asking their names and home locations as they were walking out. The Reporters interviewed more witnesses. They moved closer to the scene and showed fires breaking out in parts of the office building that had tumbled down as well as damage to buildings next to it.

On and on, the reporters covered the scene and Sara and Jake sat there watching without speaking. It was a ten story building and Peter's office was on the third floor! Neither one wanted to speak of the impossible chances that he could be alive. All they could see was rubble everywhere.

All eyes in the bar were glued to the television screen. Through the dust, they saw policemen stretching yellow crime scene tape around the area. They heard sirens wailing. They saw more people running from the scene coughing. They saw others carrying limp children. Others were limping and leaning on those who were able to walk. Chaos reigned.

They heard a reporter asking for all off duty emergency personnel to report to their work locations – firemen to fire houses, nurses and doctors to local hospitals, medi-vac personnel to their hangers and anyone with construction knowledge who could help work through the carnage to go to their offices. There was a number running along the bottom of the screen for construction workers to call if they could help. Through this number, they would be coordinated and dispatched to the scene to help.

The location of a Red Cross tent was given as names of survivors started to come in and scroll across the bottom of the screen. Neither of them saw Peter's name. Another phone number started flashing across the screen. The reporter was urging people to call the number if they suspected friends or relatives might be missing. He went on to say that the Red Cross was attempting to compile a list of people who might have been in or near the building. Sara picked up her phone and numbly dialed the number. She hit redial at least twenty times before she finally got through. The woman on the other end of the phone was patient and consoling as she gave Peter's name, address, cell phone number and firm name.

"You say he was with Jensen and Associates?" the woman asked.

"Yes."

"Just a second." Sara could hear her flipping through papers.

“That firm name sounds familiar. I think someone gave us a lot of information about that.”

The woman paused.

“Yes. Names in that firm were reported just a bit ago by a Scott Selfridge. So we already have it, but I’m afraid I have no information for you. I’m sorry.”

“But it’s still very early,” she went on. “You can leave your name and number as next of kin. That would be helpful and then we can call you right away if we hear anything.” she said encouragingly. “Don’t give up!”

“Thank you,” Sara said quietly, citing her name, relationship as Peter’s wife and phone number. “Good-bye.” But throughout the interaction, her mind was reeling. Scott was alive! He had worked with Peter for years. Surely he would know something. She hung up the phone and placed it in her handbag, almost feeling reassured. She would call him as soon as she could get home and find his number.

Several others in the bar were making the same call and they gravitated toward Sara to find solace in a group. Another woman’s husband worked in the building, a man’s son did also and another woman’s daughter not only worked there but had her granddaughter in day care in the building. She was beside herself with worry that little did they know would soon turn to grief.

The scenes on the television were riveting. Sara and Jake were glued to their bar stools, not wanting to miss a comment. A number of different people had captured the building collapse using cell phone videos and the station showed it over and over again from different angles. Special bomb analysts were called upon who pointed out that the front and right side of the building went down first. Then it was as if there were epi centers throughout where other bombs exploded, ensuring that the whole place went down. Some rattled witnesses reported hearing four separate explosions and some reported five. It was clearly a well-planned and well-executed attack.

They watched firefighters pull up and start getting water on the fires. Soon after, they started seeing wounded people pass by the cameras. Some were ambulatory. Some had to be carried. Others were on stretchers. Some stopped to talk of their harrowing escapes. Some had burns. Others had severe lacerations. Others had lost limbs. Sara and the others in the restaurant peered at the faces of the wounded and the faces of the crowd until they had eye strain.

A cheer went up when one man cried, "There's my son! There's my son!" He bought a round of drinks for others and then left to go find him. It gave Sara lots of mis-guided hope, but hope none-the-less.

Jake and Sara ended up sitting there until six pm when it all started to get repetitious and both were getting weary. Already, the scope on the scene had turned to Search and Rescue. Anyone else was not going to walk out on their own. Not surprisingly, considering the size of the blast, very few had.

Sara had fielded calls from friends, family and co-workers and continued to try to call Peter to no avail. She had also called their pet sitter, Katie, to ask if she could go over and feed Bogey (their friendly Newfoundland dog) and let him out so she could stay a little longer. Katie lived close by Sara's home and said it would be no problem. A student at a local university, she also loved Bogey and let him out whenever she could during the day while Sara and Peter were at work.

Finally, it was clear that there was nothing more to be done or for the moment, to see that might be different. Jake stood up and said, "Look Sara. Are you OK to drive home? You should probably go home because if Peter gets out safely, that's where he will go."

She jumped up. "Yes! You are so right. I have to go home now. I don't know what I was thinking. I'm sure I can find a number for Scott and I'll call him to see if he knows anything!"

"I'll follow you just to be sure you are driving OK and get there safely, OK?"

"OK" she said. "Let's go now," she added brightly, but her smile was worn. "Maybe he will already be there!"

"Yeah. Maybe," Jake replied cautiously. He felt badly because he felt certain it wouldn't be true. It couldn't be true or surely Peter would already have called. They had been waiting at the bar for hours.

Sara was shaking so she drove home slowly. She dreaded of the possibility of not finding Peter there when she arrived. But of course it proved true. When she arrived, she waved to Jake as he drove on. The house was dark and it was clear that Peter wasn't there. As usual, Bogey bounded to the door in greeting. She dropped her things and sat down on the floor, wrapping her arms around the big dog's neck. Sobbing into his fur, she said, "Where's Daddy, Bogey? Where's Daddy?"

Sara took her beloved dog for a short walk but didn't eat any dinner. Jen called and in a broken voice asked if it was really her Uncle Peter's building that had been bombed. Sara answered her matter-of-factly. Jen kept saying she was sorry over and over again until Sara said, "Well, it's way too early to tell, honey." She mustered up her courage. "I'm sure he's OK! He'll get in touch as soon as he can and I'll call you first when I hear. You know how disaster scenes are. It takes a while to sort it all out." Jen asked if she should come over, but Sara said she would rather be alone and try to get some sleep. She thanked Jen and hung up the phone, wishing she felt as confident as she had sounded.

As soon as Bogey was settled, she purposefully went to Peter's home office and rummaged on his desk for a firm telephone directory. He always kept it at his fingertips so it didn't take long to find. She sat in his chair, picked up the house phone on his desk and rang Scott Selfridge, who answered on the first ring. When she identified herself, he said, "Sara! How are you? Are you OK?"

"Yes, Scott. Well no, Scott. Actually I was wondering if you could tell me anything about Peter. Did you see him today? Was he in the building?"

"I'm so sorry to hear he hasn't come home. He must have been in the building then. I took a sick day today so I have no idea." His sympathy oozed through the telephone. "I asked my wife to take a firm directory to the Red Cross as soon as I heard. I knew it would be important for them to have everyone's name."

"I see," she said in a monotone. "Good night then. I was just checking."

"Any time, Sara. I'm so sorry. Any time. Call any time. Please let me know if there is anything at all that we can do and please let me know if you hear anything. Good night and hang in there."

Sara clenched her teeth together and hung up the house phone carefully with both hands. It was a controlled motion because her impulse was to smash the thing into the wall. Her stomach was in knots.

She got ready for bed and gratefully crawled under the covers, piling pillows all around to make a cocoon. She reached for the remote and turned on the news one more time. More volunteer tents were now being set up around Copley Square and more names were flashing along the bottom. *Thank God some people already know their loved ones are OK,* she thought. She listened to see if there was anything new while she had been driving home. At the same time, she was straining to find Peter's name on the list of survivors constantly rolling along the bottom of the screen. *Please, God,* she said out loud. *Let him be fine!* She watched the whole list scroll through and then finally fell asleep, but only for a short while. She slept fitfully, dreaming of fire and falling bricks. Peter was screaming her name but she couldn't reach him.

CHAPTER FIVE

The next morning, Sara had no illusions of going to the office. Instead, she fed Bogey and put him in his run outside; making sure his water dish was full of fresh water. He barked playfully. “Sorry, baby. I’ll walk you tomorrow,” she consoled him. “I have some things I have to do.” Then she added, “Maybe Daddy will be home soon!” Bogey agreed, barking and running around in circles in the run. “Be a good boy, now,” she said. “I’ll be back as soon as I can.”

With determination, she got into her car and drove into Boston. Jen was still on her mind, but she had more important things to think about right now. She headed to Copley Square where they had seen the reporter broadcasting last night. *Could it have been just a dream?*

As she neared Copley Square, it was clear that it was NOT a dream. This was still a good three blocks from Peter’s building but they were not letting anyone past. She tried several different ways and all were blocked off. *What could she do? She HAD to do something?* She wanted to scream. She felt so helpless and banged on the steering wheel, sobbing. *Peter! Peter, I’m so sorry! Please come home!*

The stench of dust and fire still hung in the air. It was acrid and overwhelming. She drove back to Copley Square and this time, in passing, noticed one of the volunteer tents that had been set up. *That must be the one they were talking about on the news last night,* she thought. *The main one from where they were organizing everything.* She wanted to go there. She had to go there. Maybe this was a way to get in closer and at least to stay totally on top of any information.

It took what seemed what seemed like forever to find a parking place. At least the city had been out that morning putting bags over the heads of meters to allow for free and endless parking in a show of support for what had happened, but there were many others with her same idea in mind. Others with missing loved ones. Others who wanted to gawk. Others who wanted to help.

The first place she found to park was more than a half mile away. She walked to the tent as fast as she could. The lines of volunteers wrapped around the block, but she added herself to the end and stood there, creeping slowly forward as they checked people in and gave them jobs to do. When she finally entered the tent, she saw the big white boards first. They contained lists and there were people standing by them who were responsible for keeping them updated. **LOST** (or in other words probably deceased). **MISSING. HURT WITH CURRENT LOCATION** (as in hospital, home or first aid unit) were the titles of the lists. Fire Department personnel were bringing in updates constantly and passing names and information to the volunteers. There were so many names and many of the helpers looked exhausted. *These people must have been up all night!* She thought. The list of those missing was long. She looked for Peter's name and found it there. New tears ran down her face just as her turn came to sign in.

"My husband is missing," she said. "I want to go in and help to find him."

"OK, you look strong and like you could help. You understand that this is not a pretty assignment, right?"

"Of course." She stared at him like he must be crazy.

"OK then. You won't be able to exactly go into the rubble. That's too dangerous. But you can work in the front line volunteer tent. It's close to the scene so we want everyone to have head protection just in case. Whenever you leave the tent, make sure you wear it." He directed her to the next line where she received an ID that said **VOLUNTEER** in big, red letters, a hard hat that looked more like a bicycle hat and a paper mask.

"Get on this bus" someone yelled. She did and suddenly she was on her way. *Dear God,* she prayed. *Please let me find him. One way or another. God, please just let me know what happened to him.*

CHAPTER SIX

Sara saw quickly that directing volunteers at a crime scene is not easy. It never could be because everyone had their own agenda. They were all there for a reason. Just like her, many people were looking for someone and just wanted to get near the scene. Not that they didn't want to help, but they wanted - no needed - to be nearby. *Like herding wild cats,* she thought. *Crazed cats.* But it was where she wanted to be. The only place she wanted to be.

She half listened to the lecture of a large, heavily muscled policeman speaking loudly from the front of the bus. His blue uniform was scruffy, like he hadn't changed it in a while. She suspected he had not been home since the blast and he looked tired. Twenty four hours has barely passed, so much of the scene is unsafe, he said. We need this group to work in the volunteer tent less than a block from the building. It's as close as we feel it can be safe. There, you will be helping to keep the same lists you just saw in this tent current and then helping to pass that information back here, administering first aid under the direction of doctors and nurses and keeping emergency supplies organized. We're still getting organized ourselves so there are some bugs, but please be patient.

This is where firefighters and policemen will come when they need things. Phones and more white boards have been set up. There are first aid supplies there too. Just do anything you are asked, but do NOT, I repeat DO NOT go near the rubble. Let the professionals secure the scene and work to uncover what they can in a SAFE manner. Is that understood? He sounded like a Military Commander, like he was angry. Anyone who does not follow this rule will be escorted out of here PRONTO. And believe me, no one has time for that. So keep your head down and do the job you are here to do. Keep your eye on your job at all times.

It took about twenty minutes to travel the last four and a half blocks that took them nearer the disaster scene. When they arrived, what Sara saw was actually a series of tents, all with a different purpose. Police and Firemen in neon colored vests seemed to be everywhere. They were doing every job imaginable – directing traffic, hauling victims on stretchers, throwing rubble aside and coordinating crowd control – to name only a few.

The volunteers put their badges on and filed silently off the bus. Sara thought she would gag from the dust so she put the mask over her mouth and pulled the strap behind her head. She tried to do what was asked of her, but it was so hard to concentrate. She was always watching everywhere, wanting to know what was going on everywhere – hoping for the chance of spotting Peter or anyone else from his firm – as she had been thinking all along – one way or another. The front line information boards were here and information was passed from here to the Main tent she had entered to sign up. The day passed slowly as she agonizingly watched names continue to appear on the boards. She recognized many people's names from Peter's firm on the LOST board and her heart sank.

As they worked, sounds of the recovery effort outside filled their ears. She saw the fear in the eyes of others and knew they could probably see it in her own. No one could console anyone else because they were all in the same boat. There wasn't much conversation but you could see emotion in everyone's eyes. Concern. Willingness to help. Desperation.

A large screen television had been hooked up so volunteers could see up to the minute news. As had been reported previously, it was clear that the truck bomb had not been the only blast. Several others had clearly and simultaneously come from inside the building, causing it to implode and explode at the same time, which meant that it came down extremely fast.

The hardest part was the children. They came in first because the building had blown during the recess break of a day care whose headquarters was on the first floor of the building. Specifically for people who worked there, the easy drop-off and pick-up had been a God-send for many of the working mothers. Unfortunately, it meant that the children were also involved in this horror.

The playground was right next to the building. The brick and mortar rained down so fast that there was no time to escape. A few who had been on the outskirts of the playground had superficial wounds. They were, however, traumatized by what had happened and frantic about their parents who had been in the building. Sara was with the group that cleaned wounds and bandaged these kids, then referred them to the psychologists in the next area.

One little girl in particular captured her attention. A firefighter brought her in holding her hand as she walked gingerly beside him. He was carrying another little girl in his other arm. Sara took the first little girl's hand and he then laid the other one in a corner and covered her with a sheet. Sara cringed and concentrated on the living one.

She had been told not to pick any child up before the full extent of his or her injuries was known, but since this one was ambulatory and seemed OK, she led her to a cot and helped her lie down. Her big, brown eyes were riveted on every move that Sara made. As she helped her get comfortable and covered her with a light blanket, Sara started to ask questions.

She said her name was Marta Gutenberg and that she was five years old. She was swinging on a swing near the edge of the playground when it happened. She was thrown in the air and then landed on the ground still in the swing seat. She kept repeating "still in the swing seat… still in the swing seat". Then, "Where's my mommy?"

Sara tried to speak soothingly. "I don't know, honey. Try to relax." As she spoke, she dried the girl's tears with a soft cloth she grabbed from a nearby basket. Sara was touched by the girl's innocence and saddened that something so terrible could happen to such a sweet, little soul, let alone all the others. Some of the ones on the playground had been lucky. Who knows how many were still inside the building and what their fate would be.

She was struck by Marta's resemblance to Jen, with her long, tousled, dark hair and beautiful eyes. Right down to the button nose, she could easily have been Jen's twin if they had been the same age. She was covered with dirt and the backs of her legs were skinned up with some cuts, but otherwise she seemed intact – at least physically.

Marta was covering her right ear with her right hand and said it hurt. Sara knew immediately what the problem was. She had been briefed about the blast being so loud that it had potentially blown out some people's eardrums. Marta was lucky it was only one so that she could still hear fairly well. Sara said, "OK, just hold on a minute. Sit right here and don't move, OK?"

The girl nodded while Sara went to get a warm compress from the First Aid section as well as some bandages. When she returned, she showed Marta how to hold the compress against her ear while she cleaned and bandaged her legs.

"You're a lucky little girl! I don't even think you're going to need any stitches and your ear will heal with time."

The girl stuck out her lower lip. "Where's my Mommy? she asked. "Where's my Daddy?"

Sara asked hesitantly. "Did they both work in the building?

"Yes, and I want them now," she whined.

"I'm sure you do, but we're going to have to wait a bit honey. Where are your grandparents?"

“All gone. My Daddy’s Mommy and Daddy died a long time ago and my Mommy’s died last year. In a car crash.” She started to cry.

Sara was appalled. This little girl had already been through so much. She tried to keep her voice as calm as possible. “Just lie down and try to rest for a few minutes, OK?”

“OK,” Marta said sadly and settled into the cot, pulling the blanket up over her ears.

A medic came by to give Marta a mild sedative. Sara patted her on the arm and went to help others. When she checked back a half an hour later, Marta was still in the same position, fast asleep.

Most were not so lucky. Many were brought in on gurneys and moved to the floor in another tent that had become a makeshift morgue. There, they were tagged, photographed and examined for anything that might serve as identification. Relatives of the kids were also milling around and another team was needed to help to handle their grief. To Sara, it was like a war scene in a movie. She knew she would never be able to forget it.

Throughout the day, they kept hearing loud noises from shifting of the building that had become rubble. Sometimes it was a loud crash when an unstable section let go. Each new noise made everyone jump, especially the victims lying on the cots or standing around. You could look into their eyes and imagine them re-living their terror. Those that were able would rush to the television to see what had happened. Cameras trained on the scene immediately reported what had happened with a blow by blow description and its possible consequences. At times, Sara wished they would turn it off so she could concentrate. Most of the time though, she too would stop, train an ear on the television's sound and listen. Always looking for news, for something to hang on to, for hope.

With each loud noise, she imagined someone who had been trapped alive and terrified up until that point meeting their Maker.

At one point she ran into the gruff looking policeman who had ordered her off the bus. "See? He said. "That's why we can't let just anyone near that building yet. Now do you believe me?"

"I always believed you. We always believed you." She patted his arm. "We were just in shock."

He nodded and walked away.

Each morning, Sara returned, unable to stay away. At the end of the third day, hopes of finding people alive were growing slim. Most of the names were going on the growing list on the LOST board as people were uncovered or pieces of them were found and identified. She scoured the list whenever she could, as well as another list of belongings that had been either simply listed or matched to their owners.

Despite the stench in the tent that had been set up to hold bodies and recovered belongings, she also made sure she walked through that twice a day. No Peter. No Peter anywhere. Nothing that even belonged to him that she could find.

Coming out of her assigned tent on the fourth evening, Sara ran into a policeman on his way in. It was Moe, a large, kind hearted fellow who had once been her personal body guard. They had been good friends ever since. Moe had obviously been working hard and looked disheveled. His uniform was smeared with dirt and his hands were dirty. His nails were torn. He had clearly been helping to dig through the rubble. He tried to smile at Sara, but he had seen more death and destruction than his big heart could stand. He simply held out his arms and she responded with a heartfelt hug.

They held each other for thirty seconds before he finally spoke. “I almost hate to bring it up, but is there any sign of Peter?”

“No, not yet,” she said. “But I’m holding out hope. It has only been three days and you know… miracles happen.”

“Yes, miracles happen. Let’s keep hoping. I’m watching for him too. What floor was his office on again?”

“Three.”

“Oh,” he said. Simply “Oh”. His shoulders sagged and he looked away. “Hang in there, Sara.” “It’s bad out there,” was all he could muster.

She nodded. As if she didn’t already know that.

They gave each other a resigned smile and she said, “Good to see you, Moe. You hang in there too.” She was sure his job was much worse than hers. She could hardly imagine what he was going through.

“I’m out there in the middle of the rubble, Sara. If I find anything you’ll be the first to know. I promise,” he offered.

Sara creased her eyebrows and nodded, her sadness deepening. The truth was that her hope was waning. The only good in this whole mess was Marta. A make-shift orphanage had been set up in a nearby house with Volunteers taking care of the children, and collecting donated clothing, food and other things they needed. There were about twenty children who had survived and it would take time to get them placed in homes. In the meantime, counselors had been brought in to help the little ones deal with their individual situations.

Each evening, Sara stopped by to see Marta. She always took her something. A piece of candy. A picture book. A cupcake. Each time, Marta asked about her parents, but she was starting to get wise and realize they were probably not coming back. On this particular night, she was very clingy. Sara was reading her a book when she blurted out, "What if they don't find my Mommy and my Daddy?" she said tearfully. "Will YOU be my mommy?"

Sara was taken aback. *How could she respond?* She held the little girl in her arms, rocking back and forth in the chair. "Oh honey," she said. "I'm so sorry."

The woman in charge of the make shift orphanage was stout with a name to match - Josie Boulder. Although she looked rough, her heart was as big as her name. She was in the kitchen starting dinner when Sara stopped by to check out. Visitors were screened and close track was kept of in and out times for visitations.

Josie had just turned on the television. A news alert flashed across the screen. SUSPECTS IDENTIFIED. Drawings of two male faces and two female faces filled the screen. Sara sat down to watch more and memorized the faces. They seemed to be middle-eastern, but it was hard to tell. Everyone expected that these days and she knew better than to jump to conclusions. No matter the ethnicity, there was something horrifying about seeing the pictures. To think there were people out there who could cause this kind of suffering to so many people – to anyone at all, was unimaginable. Their audacity was incomprehensible.

The faces were police mockups. The male faces came from descriptions from a number of people who saw a man running from a large van parked in front of the building and another man driving a blue Cadillac who sped in and picked him up. The others came from a person who had seen two suspiciously acting women as she had left the building about a half an hour before the blast. There was also surveillance video that seemed to indicate that the women had entered the building to plant the inside bombs together about an hour before the truck pulled up in front so the bombs could be timed to go off simultaneously. Luckily the control room for the surveillance had been off site so the tapes were available and subject to immediate review. Sara sat for an hour numbly watching and re-watching this latest information before she finally got up to go home. No group had claimed responsibility for the bombing. She was disappointed in this because she desperately wanted to place blame. She needed someone to hate. She signed out to leave. Whoever they were, she hated them all the way home.

Each night, there was a message on her answering machine from Jen as well as one from Jen's mom, her only sister, Corinne. They were full of sympathy, questions about news of Peter and questions about what they could possibly do to help.

Her sister had divorced about five years earlier and then a year later married George Henley, a strapping guy from Minnesota that she had met skiing in Europe. They had moved to Duluth after the wedding. The sisters didn't see each other very often due to the distance and had seemed to grow apart, but Corinne wanted to know when- not if – she should come to help. They were still sisters and that counted for a lot. It was time to re-connect and she wanted to support Sara in this difficult time. Sara tried once to call each of them back but didn't get an answer on either phone. Most nights she was just too exhausted to try. She didn't really care either. She just wanted to be alone. She could never quite get Peter out of her mind, especially at night. Every night, she thought about him, always the good and never the bad. She suddenly couldn't remember anything bad at all. Not an event. Not a feeling. Not a word. Sometimes she smiled as she remembered, but most of the time she cried.

Sara was having enough trouble handling her raging emotions without anyone else around. At the moment, Bogey was enough.

CHAPTER SEVEN

On the tenth day after the bombing, Sara finally went back to the office. She walked into the middle of a nasty argument between Jen and Patsy. Not caring to know the reason, she simply held up her hands for them to stop, which they did immediately. Jen threw up her hands also and humbly said, "Sorry." Then they all walked off in different directions.

Sara was in a bad mood. She really didn't want to see or talk to anyone. Luckily they didn't bug her and let her sit in her office alone until lunchtime. Her denial about Peter turned to anger revolving around every aspect of the horrible assault on his building and the people who worked there. She was irrationally angry at him for leaving and she was angry with herself for not being able to do anything about the situation. Instead of going for lunch, at noon she got up to close her door when she heard singing. She cringed and looked at the date on her watch - July 18.

"Happy Birthday to you, Happy Birthday to yoooooou, Happy Birthday Dear Sara, Happy Birthday to you!"

She had totally forgotten that today was her birthday. She would have preferred to ignore it, but there they were – the whole office right in her face. Patsy balanced a cake on her left hand as she walked, shielding the candles with her right so they wouldn't blow out. Behind her, the assistant office manager, Jimmy Frank led a Congo line that included everyone in the office. Bringing up the tail end were Jen, Laura and Susan. They were all laughing, singing and swaying to the music they were making. One investment advisor was playing the Happy Birthday song on a flutophone and a research analyst was playing wild arpeggios on a harmonica. Their eyes were wide and their expressions exaggerated in an attempt to cheer her up. People with high stress jobs tend to get a little crazy when they have a chance to let down and she couldn't help but burst out laughing.

Certainly Jimmy and Patsy had colluded to organize this. Jimmy looked like a very tall, skinny Pee Wee Herman, with a mane of thick, jet black hair and a personality to match. His big, round eyes were lit up as he waved his arms, directing the song. It was impossible to be sad or grumpy around Jimmy. He did everything with gusto and his enthusiasm was always contagious. He was always telling jokes, running lottery tickets or planning a party. She had to admit that it was he who diligently kept their office life in perspective.

The cake was ceremoniously placed on her desk. It was beautiful. They all knew how Sara loved frosting and the whole thing was covered with big, red and white frosting roses. She was tempted to take the accompanying knife and scrape the whole top off and onto her plate. Instead she blew out the candles in one puff – even though there were 45 of them. That garnered much applause. Then they really surprised her. Each person had a little gift and they filed by to present them.

"What? she exclaimed. "This is way too much! Why are you doing this? This is really out of line!" For a second she felt angry again. She had work to do! This would take way too much time. She looked nervously at Jake but he seemed fine, so she squashed the thoughts and laughed and smiled as she opened all twenty-five of them.

The gifts were cute and thoughtful – a miniature Newfoundland statue to remind her of her dog, Bogey, to keep on her desk, funny office supplies and perfume. Patsy gave her some wildly colored post-it notes and Jake gave her a beautiful scarf. Then finally came the last three – the firm's compliance officers. George Lucas had a large bag of ice, John Banfield had an 8-pack of Diet Pepsi and Chuck Pentley had a huge bottle of Captain Morgan rum. "We thought we would all join you with your obvious drink of choice. Skinny Pirates all around," he yelled and began pouring.

"Oh my God," she said. "It's a good thing Jake is participating because it looks like we're not getting much done the rest of the day." She grabbed the pen she had been using and threw it up in the air.

Jake laughed and she had to admit, the whole production did make her feel somewhat normal again – if only for a short while.

Chuck poured a glass heavy on rum and Sara's eyes teared up. "This was really, really sweet guys. I can't thank you enough." She picked up her glass, held it in the air and said "CHEERS!"

Just then a delivery guy showed up with foot long subs. Sara was grateful for that and only had one drink, albeit a stiff one, as did most everyone else. Chairs were dragged in and they stayed several hours – all together – not only her co-workers but clearly her friends. She had to drive home in four hours and knew that more would give her a rip-roaring headache as well as having to pay for a cab ride home.

Finally she clapped her hands and called out "OK. Enough!"

Jake jumped up and added, "Right, back to work!"

Was it Sara's imagination or did he seem slightly relieved? She watched him out of the corner of her eye, hoping he was not upset to have an entire afternoon of work vanish before his eyes. She knew he wanted her to have a moment of happiness. She knew he felt sorry for her. But after all, he had a firm to run!

When they all finally left, she couldn't concentrate and the anger flared up again. She was still mad at Peter for dying. She was mad about being alone. She was mad at the world for nothing. She picked up her pen again and threw it at the wall.

Later as she was on her way to drop some papers on Chuck's desk, she glanced in the break room as she passed. Laura and Susan (Jen's friends) were in there, whispering over cups of coffee. On an impulse, she walked in, smiling and saying hi to the girls. They immediately stopped talking and the air was unbearably brittle as Sara tried to nonchalantly pour herself a cup of coffee. When she turned back to the girls, she thought they looked nervous.

"So," she started out. "How are you guys? Everything going OK around the office?"

Both simply nodded, so she continued. "I've been meaning to ask you. Do you think Jen is OK? Is there anything I should know about?"

Both shook their heads and unconsciously took a step backward.

Sara put her head down slightly and looked up at them both sternly. “Are you sure?”

“Absolutely,” they said in tandem. Then they laughed. “Great minds think alike!” chortled Laura as they both scurried out.

Returning to her office, Sara couldn’t help but laugh at herself. *Bright, really bright,* she thought. *Asking them when they were together was brilliant. I can’t believe I expected to find anything out from those two.*

She worked after hours again and was surprised when she looked up and saw Laura at her door. She knocked on the doorframe of Sara’s office and sheepishly said, “May I come in?”

“Sure! Of course! What’s up?”

“I didn’t want to say anything in front of Susan. I didn’t want her to think I was ratting Jen out, but I AM worried about her. I really am. She doesn’t seem herself these days. It’s like she thinks she’s Nancy Drew and she’s spending a lot of time with Mr. Smythe.”

"What do you mean by a lot of time? She's an intern here just like you and she's supposed to help everybody."

"I know, but it's like she takes every opportunity to go into his office whether he's there or not. I asked her and she told me she's looking for something, but she wouldn't tell me what it is. I know they've gone out to dinner together too. Don't you think that's funny?"

"Maybe." Sara twirled her pen thoughtfully. "You don't think she has a crush on him or anything, do you? He's quite a bit older than she is to say the least."

"No, I don't really think that. I wish I could give you more details. It makes me feel funny saying anything because I don't have them. It's just a funny feeling. It isn't quite right. I feel like there's something going on. I'm sorry."

"Oh heavens. Don't be sorry. You're a great friend to worry about her and I appreciate your coming to me. I'll talk to Jen about it and straighten it all out."

"Please don't tell her I said anything!"

"Of course not. Don't worry. I'll find a way to speak to her that won't implicate you at all. Really, don't worry. I promise." Sara smiled reassuringly.

"OK." Laura backed out of the room hesitantly. "I trust you. Please don't forget that."

Sara smiled again. "I won't."

Sara had every intention of talking to Jen the next morning. However, she had forgotten that Jen was leaving for a week's vacation, so now it would be a while before she had her chance.

CHAPTER EIGHT

Three weeks after the bombing of Peter's building, Sara's desk phone rang. It was Patsy. "Sara," she said, hesitating. "Moe is here. You know, your friend who is the policeman? He wants to talk to you." A full moment of silence passed as Sara's heart dropped through the floor. Then she replied softly, "OK. Send him in."

She looked up at Moe when he entered but didn't get up. Her legs felt too weak. She had always called him the Gentle Giant and he had the sweetest, most sympathetic look on his face. It was unnerving and tears started to glisten in her eyes. She knew it had to be bad news.

Moe walked over and gently placed a torn wallet on her desk. Then he sat down as Sara registered what it was. Peter's wallet. Torn but intact. She reached out and touched it, her heart beating rapidly and her fingers lingering on the well-worn leather. Moe sat down and simply watched as she picked it up and looked inside. Everything was there. She saw all of Peter's credit cards. She pulled out his driver's license and looked at the picture, then completely dissolved into a massive attack of tears. As she sobbed, Moe still just sat there, showing his support through his silence.

"I'm sorry, Sara... Mrs. Jensen" he finally said. "I'm afraid this is proof that your husband was in the building." He waited for that thought to register and then continued. "Sara, there's one more thing." He pulled a watch out of his pocket and handed it to her. It was a Breitling with a dark blue face and a silver band. The face was shattered and the time had stopped at 12:30 pm – the exact time of the blast. She stared at the face, and then turned it over, already knowing the worst. There was the inscription. *To my beloved Peter on our wedding day, 1-1-79.*

"Sara, I have to tell you that we may never find anything more. Peter's office was on the third floor, so seven floors above that came crashing down on top of it. Crushed is really an understatement. What's left is... well... unrecognizable. The only reason these things survived is that they were wedged in a gap between two pieces of cement."

"Some things were actually blown outside– like the watch there. It was found about a half a block away," he went on. "Things were scattered and also crushed. It's just a very difficult scene in terms of any identification."

"But there must be bodies," she said.

"Yes and no," he replied softly. There are pieces of bodies. We may or may not be able to identify them. Regardless, it will take a long time."

She continued to cry as he spoke, grabbing Kleenex out of a drawer and intermittently blowing her nose. "I had still hoped," she finally said. "Hoped beyond hope I guess. I have missed him so much. I feel so guilty because that last night we hardly spoke to each other. I wasn't the best wife and I really let him down." She looked at Moe with mascara streaking her face. "I did really love him. I wish I had told him that every single day. Every single minute."

"I'm sure Peter knew you loved him, Sara," Moe said quietly. "He loved you very much too. But you're going to have to move on now. I'm so sorry." When she didn't answer, he got up and left quietly.

After he left, Sara's guilt was overwhelming. She still couldn't face Peter's death, although it was clearly a reality. She hadn't been going to church lately, but still she tried to bargain with God. *If only you will send him back and say it wasn't true, I'll be a better person. If only I had been nicer to him. If only I had been a better wife. If only… if only… if only.*

She tried for a full hour but couldn't get any more work done. Placing Peter's wallet and watch in her briefcase, she decided to head home. She said good-bye to Patsy and mentioned that she was stopping to see Marta. Patsy smiled, sensing how important Marta was becoming to her boss. She was glad that Sara was finding some solace in the girl, even if Sara didn't realize it.

As Sara was driving, she bargained with God. *Please let him be all right. Please send him back and I promise to be a better wife!*

She was cheered up only by the thought of stopping to see Marta. Mrs. Boulder had gotten her a new dress and she was excitedly twirling around to show Sara how pretty she felt. Her smile was so exuberant. Sara took her picture and gave her a big hug. She stayed an hour then, sitting with the little girl and reading books. When it came time to leave, it tore at her heart.

When she arrived at home, Sara quickly changed into a running suit, leashed Bogey and went for a run. She ran hard and fast, oblivious to everyone and everything. Once they ran out in front of a car. She didn't even realize it until she heard the screeching breaks. Luckily it was a miss – a near one, but a miss. A little more mindfully now, she ran on until she could run no more and Bogey was pulling on the leash to slow down. They walked home slowly – both panting. She had only one thought. *How will I go on?*

Bogey was hungry when they arrived back home. She fed him, let him out in the back yard for a few minutes and then back in. He headed up for a big, soft dog bed in the corner of her bedroom. She followed, laid down beside him, put her arm around the big dog and fell asleep.

CHAPTER NINE

As much as Sara didn't want to, it was time to start thinking about planning a funeral. She called Patsy and begged off coming in, saying she would work from home and to call her if anything came up. Jen – just back from vacation - found out Sara was at home and after work drove over without calling. She didn't want to give Sara a chance to say no. She found her with piles of pictures and photo albums spread out on the table in the breakfast nook off of the kitchen. Sara had been looking slowly at photo after photo, reminiscing about each one in turn, wallowing in memories of times together with Peter.

Jen had picked up some BBQ chicken wraps, which Sara was glad to see. She hadn't eaten any breakfast or lunch and was suddenly hungry. Jen picked up a half bottle of Carlisle Zinfandel that had been re-corked and was sitting on the counter. She poured two glasses and put the wraps on plates. As they ate, they looked through the pictures together. It was comforting having Jen there – not as easy a task as Sara had thought it would be because each picture held a memory. Each one cried out to be discussed. Some were bittersweet – pictures of them with family members who had passed, but after a while, they did find some to giggle at. They discarded some, saved the best and made sure to include funny pictures of Peter – in Halloween costumes, clowning for the camera on vacation trips, pictures with Jen when she was a baby.

"May I have this one after the funeral, Aunt Sara?" Sara looked up. It was a picture of Peter holding Jen up in the air when she was about four years old. The look exchanged between them was priceless."

"Of course, honey," she said softly. "Of course that can be yours." A tear trickled down her cheek and she quickly wiped it away. The picture meant even more because it could easily have been Marta. The resemblance was uncanny.

There were piles and piles of pictures. It got so late that Jen decided to stay over in the guest room.

The next morning, Sara called to make an appointment with the Funeral Director and then printed more recent pictures of Peter that she had in digital form. She and Jen picked up pictures she had in frames around the house, putting them in boxes to take to the funeral home. It was comforting having Jen around. She suddenly couldn't remember why she had been so aloof. At that point, company was good. Jen called her mom and they both encouraged Corinne to fly in the next day so she would be there for the funeral.

Jen came along to the appointment at the funeral home and Sara was relieved because getting through it was a lot harder than she had expected. Jen kept her sane as they worked through the details and planned a fitting memorial for her husband. She left the pictures to be arranged around the reception room during the wake, which would take place in two days with no visitation beforehand. She knew she was not up to that.

When they were finished and heading home in her car, Sara finally had a chance to talk to Jen about Patsy's observation. She knew it would be a difficult conversation and didn't really know where to start, so she just blurted it out.

"I need to talk to you about a different subject, Jen. I don't know how to say this any other way than to be completely honest. I've got to get something off my chest."

Jen looked worried. "What, Aunt Sara? Did I do something wrong? Is everything OK?"

"I hope not. I mean, I can't imagine this is true, but Patsy has accused you of stealing from petty cash. She also says the other girls – the other interns – are jealous of you because you are getting special favors. Frankly, I'm not sure what she meant by that because I certainly haven't given any and haven't seen any."

Jen looked incredulous and was immediately defensive. "That lying b…"

"Jen! Watch your language! I've got enough on my mind without escalating this."

"But Aunt Sara! She's off her rocker! You think you know Patsy, but she's mean and devious and she thinks she runs the place. She makes my life very difficult because she's jealous of my relationship with Greg Smythe!"

"What? What relationship? You have a RELATIONSHIP with Greg Smythe?"

"No. No. No. Not really. She has a vivid imagination and her jealousy is really getting in the way."

"Does Patsy have a relationship with him?"

"I don't know for sure, but it sure seems like it. If I had to guess I'd say she's head over heels in love with him."

"Really." Sara was quiet and thoughtful for a few minutes. She certainly had not seen any indication of this – only arguments that made her think Patsy didn't care for Greg.

She went on. "I find that really hard to believe, but he is a handsome, intelligent guy so I guess it's possible."

"Not only possible. It's real. Open your eyes, Aunt Sara!"

"OK, Jen. You know that office romance is strictly verboten, right?"

"Yes, I do and so does Patsy for sure. That has to be the reason that she has been hiding it from you."

"OK. I'll look into it. But in the meantime, please tell me that her accusation is false."

Jen looked hurt and then spoke forcefully. "I can't believe you would even ask me that, but yes, it's completely false. I never went near the petty cash. She must be stealing it herself and trying to blame me so you won't suspect her. And as far as the other interns, they are just jealous too. I do get a lot of good projects, but it's because I'm good at them, not because I get any special favors. If they would work a little harder, they would get them too." She was defensive and pouting. "They're all trying to sabotage me and I'm getting sick of it! I'm glad you finally know."

Sara wanted to believe her niece under any circumstances. "I'm sorry, Jen. I didn't realize this had been going on for a while. All right. I'll look into it, OK? Just give me a few more days and let me get through this funeral first."

CHAPTER TEN

Corinne did fly in the next day. Sara was able to maintain a brave face until she actually saw her sister. Corinne had always been her closest friend on earth and she could never deceive her. Once the tears were dried and they were on their way home, Sara felt buoyed up. Jen usually flew home to visit her mom and Sara hadn't seen her sister for almost a year. Despite that, time immediately vanished and it was as if they had seen each other the day before. It was wonderful to have her to talk to. With their parents already gone, Sara knew she could always count on her sister's solid advice. How could she have thought that they had grown apart?

Corinne looked great. She had been working out, lightened her hair and the happiness of her new marriage showed. Corinne was only two years younger and in the past, people had often confused them for twins. But when Sara looked in the mirror she thought it appeared now that there was more like ten years between them. *Why had she let herself go? When had she aged so much? No wonder Peter had been unhappy.*

Sara confessed this to Corinne who immediately jumped to her defense. She came close and put her hands on Sara's shoulders, slightly shaking them. “Why are you beating yourself up?” she demanded. “Snap out of it! You are beautiful inside and out. Why are you doing this to yourself? Was there something going on between you and Peter that I didn’t know about?”

Sara choked and started crying again. Then it all came out. She told Corinne about how she and Peter had grown apart and stopped spending much time together. She told her why she thought it was all her fault. She told her how sorry she was and how she had had a plan to try to make it better.

Corinne looked troubled. “I saw a bit of this when I was here last. I wish I had talked to you about it then. Maybe I could have helped. I’m sorry.”

She was silent for a few minutes, choosing her words carefully. “You know, Sara. Everything usually works out for the best. I know you can’t really compare this to a divorce, but try to understand what I am trying to explain to you.” She put her hands on Sara’s shoulders and emphasized the words again. “Things most always work out for the best. When I went through my divorce, I thought it was the worst thing in the world. But now I see that I’m happier than I’ve ever been. I just didn’t know what I was missing.”

She paused, looking directly into Sara’s eyes. Then she said softly, “This happiness can also be yours.

You're looking at only the good now, but maybe you couldn't have salvaged what you had with Peter. Maybe you should spend some time thinking about the bad parts of that marriage. Maybe there's someone out there who's better for you than Peter was. You said you were unhappy as well."

She paused, giving Sara a chance to speak. But Sara just looked at her, thinking deeply about what her sister was saying. Since she could see that Sara was really listening, Corinne went on. "Please stop dwelling on the past. Please try to accept this as some kind of divine intervention or whatever you believe in. I'm sure it was meant to be. I'm also sure it will be all right."

Sara nodded but said, "I know you mean well, and I really see the difference in you because of your happiness, but this is all really hard to think about right now." Her brow was furrowed.

"Well, a lot of that is acceptance of myself you know. You can't grow happiness by planting seeds in other people. You tried to do that with Peter. You're still trying. But believe me; you have to plant those seeds in yourself."

"I know." Sara nodded. "I know you're right. I'll work on that."

"Hey, maybe you should start going to church again, Sara. And while you're at it, why don't you take Jen with you?"

Sara laughed. "Right. Jen would only do that to support me and she has enough problems of her own."

"What do you mean? Enough problems of her own? What problems?"

Sara immediately regretted her words. She wasn't ready to talk to Corinne about Jen and actually, she wasn't really sure what was going on. It wasn't appropriate and she didn't want any confrontation. Corinne would go straight to Jen and it would ruin her relationship with her niece. She stuttered. "Uh… y… y… you know. At her age, there are all kinds of issues. Like trying to sort out your life and what you really want to do. You know." Luckily Corinne accepted that.

"OK. Let's let it be for now. At least think about a support group. And always know that I'm here for you to lean on. You can call me any time and let's not let so much time pass between visits, OK?"

"OK."

They both smiled and simultaneously threw their arms around each other.

Sara was very happy to have her sister at her side during the funeral. The planning had been harder than she had expected but the actual event was even harder.

To Sara's surprise, the funeral was a sea of people. So many of their friends and co-workers turned out. Jake was unobtrusive but nearby through the whole thing. She could see that he and their closest friends were grieving deeply. Peter had been well liked and thought of as an honorable and exemplary person. Many came forward to speak and made that perfectly clear. She was flooded with memories as many shared their favorite moments with him or with them as a couple.

There were also a number of people there that Sara didn't know. For some reason, one in particular troubled her. He was a large Italian man who sat in the back pew during the service. She noticed him when she walked down the aisle of the church – the same aisle she had walked down to take Peter's hand in marriage. She simply felt funny about him – like he was scrutinizing her. He wasn't there at the end and she wrote it off to her fragile and emotional state. *Surely I'm making things up,* she thought. So many people were approaching her with condolences that she soon forgot about it.

She was especially glad Corinne was there because of Jen, who was taking Peter's death very hard. Jen had always been his little princess. He had spoiled her rotten and was always trying to think of fun events to take her to. Jen had adored him.

But Jen wasn't thinking of herself. She was thinking of her aunt. *What would it be like to love and be married to someone for twenty five years and then to suddenly lose them?* Jen knew her aunt and uncle had lots of good – no great – friends who would be there for her, but she also knew it would never be the same. She was sorrier for her aunt than for herself.

Corinne was an absolute saint. Sara watched her swallowing her own grief and switching into mother mode for Jen and protection mode for Sara, pulling her away from conversations when she saw Sara was struggling. Corinne guided her through, making sure that everyone got their turn to speak, but never letting anyone get overwhelming. Sara would be indebted to her forever.

Corinne was sad for her sister because she had no children for comfort and support. She was glad she had her Jen at least and that Sara was nearby now that she lived so far away.

For obvious reasons, there was no graveside service. Sara waited until the crowd dispersed and the Funeral Director had put several bouquets she had chosen to take home in her car. She left the rest to be used for regular church services and to be distributed to senior homes in the area.

While she was sorting out the flowers, Corinne had taken Sara's car keys and pulled the car up. Finally resting her head on the passenger side, Sara sighed in relief. At least this was now behind her. Hopefully somehow she could find the strength to move on.

Funeral home personnel followed her home and helped her place the flowers she had chosen around the house. She had kept most of the roses – her favorites – and there was a bouquet for every room. She had avoided the ones that looked specifically like funeral sprays in an attempt to keep the house as cheerful as it could be. The pictures were in bags that were stowed in cupboards in the breakfast room. She knew she was not ready to put them back out. She would have to spend the time going through them again to choose the perfect ones to keep. Pictures that would be friendly but not excruciating reminders.

Corrine stayed for three days. She helped Sara sort through Peter's things and was a genuine comfort. Jen hung around a lot also to be with her mother and there were times when they almost had fun.

Sara and Jen drove Corinne to the airport together. The sisters promised each other never to let so much time pass before they were together again. The good-byes were difficult. The loss of Peter made them both want to hold everyone dear to them close and to keep them safe. If only it were possible.

Jen dropped Sara at home where she fed Bogey and then flipped on the kitchen television. She almost dropped Bogey's bowl when she saw **NEWS FLASH** across the bottom of the screen. The two women bombers had been on the run for months, but there they were on the screen - captured! She watched as one was being led to a police car. She was a tall, homely girl with brown hair, wearing a red headband and big glasses. She had on a plaid skirt and a black lacey top – just like any other young woman in Wellesley her age could have worn. Nothing made her stand out. Her hands were handcuffed behind her back and she was screaming at the policeman in Spanish.

The other woman also looked young. She was thin and dressed similarly. She seemed tall too, but she was lying on the ground with her back to the camera. All Sara could see was a mass of black hair lying in a pool of blood. A big, black bag had been zipped open and laid out. She watched as two policemen lifted her body over onto the bag. They zipped it up and she was gone from view. Even though the woman was probably a terrorist, it was chilling to watch.

The phone rang and it was Jake. “Sara, have you got your television on?”

“Just now. I’m looking at the news in shock. What a great day for them to get the two women bombers. This finally gives me some closure.”

“Can you believe how long they’ve been out there right under our noses? Apparently they were pretty good at hiding in plain sight!” He was chuckling.

“Yeah. Shopping in a cheese shop in Wellesley. Good thing somebody was paying attention. I wouldn’t have expected them to be in such an affluent place either. I don’t know why. I just didn’t.”

“I know. It’s wild. It just goes to show you that you’ve always got to be vigilant no matter where you are.”

“It does make you wonder who’s in the car next to you, who’s shopping next to you, who your encounters are really with.” She shook her head. “It’s crazy!”

“They did try to disguise themselves – different hair color and a haircut, glasses, colored contacts under them – but it sure is brassy for them to be right out in public like that. I would have expected them to be thousands of miles away by now. They’ve been right here all this time! I just can’t get over it.”

“So what exactly happened? I see one in handcuffs and one lying on the ground.”

“Evidently the two of them were walking out of the shop when the police pulled up. One woman pulled out a gun and started shooting. There’s one wounded cop who was already taken away in an ambulance. The police took the armed one out and the other one tried to run but another police car pulled up and she didn’t even make it out of the parking lot.

“Wow, that’s great. I’ll sleep well tonight!”

“Do sleep well, but I’m sure there are more wackos out there. Always keep up your vigilance. You never know.”

“OK, Jake. Thanks for calling! See you tomorrow.”

“See you tomorrow, Sara. Hang in there. Everything is going to be all right.”

As she hung up the phone, she prayed he and Corinne were correct.

CHAPTER ELEVEN

Sara thought long and hard about what Corinne had said about attending a support group. She knew that most people who needed help didn't see it themselves and the fact that she could made her sure she should give it a try. Coincidentally, she had picked up several cards in the volunteer tent for group and individual help. There were many firms who had set up classes and appointment times especially for relatives of bombing victims. At the time she picked them up she thought she would give them to others, but they were still in her purse so she pulled them out. How to choose one? She knew that getting into a group that was right for her was important. She knew she should probably ask around but she didn't want anyone to know. She wanted them all to think she was fine – that she didn't need any help.

She peered at the cards. The names told her nothing, so she chose one by address. There was one meeting two blocks away from her office. That would at least be convenient.

The first night, Sara entered the door hesitantly. She looked around, praying there wasn't anyone there she knew. It was a group meeting. Chairs were arranged in a circle with a round coffee table in the middle. Kleenex boxes were conveniently arranged around the table. *Oh God,* she thought. The last thing I need is a cry fest.

She forced herself to go in. She took a chair with empty chairs on both sides so she didn't have to talk to anyone. Within ten minutes, however, the chairs will full so it didn't matter anyway. She stared straight ahead, but the woman on her right was insistent in introducing herself. "Hi, I'm Geannie with a G," she said.

Sara gave her a half smile that was actually more of a lip pursing. "Hi, I'm Sara."

Geannie with a G started on about how she had lost her son and granddaughter in the building explosion.

"Oh," Sara murmured. "I'm so sorry."

"How about you?" she went on.

"I don't really want to talk about it."

"But isn't that why we're here?"

Sara gave her another pursed lip smile. "I'm not sure. We'll see."

Geannie took the cue and left her alone. Sara was ready to bolt already. *Why had she come to a group session instead of an individual one?* Luckily the group leader came in a few moments later and put her out of her misery. She glued herself to her seat and buttoned her lip.

Unfortunately it only lasted a few minutes. The friendly group leader expressed her sorrow at everyone's loss and outlined the five steps of grief – Denial/Isolation, Anger, Bargaining, Depression and Acceptance. That was fine, but then she started around the room and asked everyone to say their name and reveal why they were there. Sara had been hoping it wouldn't be like this, but actually wasn't surprised. Isn't that how group therapy worked? You get it all out and then talk about it? The leader clearly sensed from Sara's attitude rigid stare and coldness that she would lose her if she didn't immediately draw her in, so she called on her first.

"Hi. I'm Sara Jensen," she said rigidly. "My husband is missing. Dead. He was in the building. I think you all know what building I'm talking about. The City Centre. I… I don't know how he died. I just know he died and… like the rest of you I'm sure… I'm here because I'm having trouble dealing with it."

Sympathetic murmurs could be heard around the room. She didn't look up to see where they were coming from. She didn't say anymore. She was suddenly a little curious about where she was in the grieving process but she didn't really care. What difference did it make?

After a short pause, the leader said sweetly, "OK, Sara. That's fine. You don't have to say any more. We are so sorry for your loss. Geannie, would you like to go next?"

Geannie was ready and chomping at the bit. She had a lot to say. Tearfully, she described the loss of her son and granddaughter. Her son's body had not been recovered, but she had a lot of detail about how her granddaughter was killed outside on the playground. She was covered with cuts and bruises from flying debris and one piece had deeply pierced her in the head. People around the circle teared up and murmured their sympathy. Sara wondered if she had seen her in the makeshift morgue.

It got worse from there. Several people were crying so hard by the time it was their turn that they couldn't speak. A lot of that Kleenex got used. By the time all ten others had had at least a chance to speak, Sara was heartsick. Her seat felt molded to her body and she wondered if she could stand.

The leader gave a short speech trying to encourage everyone. She said all wrongs have some positive somewhere and the assignment for next week was to find something positive that had come or would come from the loss that each of us had incurred.

Sara stood up weakly, said a polite good-bye to Geannie and left the room. As she headed to her car she thought, *What could possibly be positive about this?* And she never went back. She had enough of her own problems. Knowing about the problems of others just didn't seem to help. In fact, it made it worse. It was more to feel sorry about. More to feel badly about. More to mourn and she needed to move on as quickly as she could.

Sara was looking for reasons not to go home. Bogey was well taken care of by Katie and it was getting more and more difficult to be there because everything in the house reminded her of Peter. Instead of dissipating, the feeling seemed to be getting stronger and more disturbing.

The next night she went to a museum. Perhaps she could lose herself in the paintings. At first, being at the museum did calm her. She went to her favorite paintings first. As she stood in front of "The Nut Gatherers" by Adolphe Bouguereau, she could clearly see the surprise and excitement passing between the two girls sitting among the trees. She imagined one telling the other a secret and that made her think about the therapy sessions.

Standing there thinking about it, it seemed to Sara that each individual has to find his or her own therapy in their own way. Knowing everyone else's misery certainly didn't help. She suddenly felt like people should keep their secrets to themselves. She could also easily imagine the other girl in the painting running off and telling someone else the secret who would tell someone else who would tell someone else – and there it would be – out there for everyone to see. She just wanted to bury the whole ugly mess and start over. It certainly wasn't going to help to share her feelings with a group. Or maybe she just wasn't ready for that. She didn't know.

Normally she loved hanging out at the museum and it was relaxing time, always well spent. She used to think most people in the paintings looked happy or at least indifferent. But now she saw sadness everywhere. If only she could even get to the point of feeling indifferent maybe it could be enough.

CHAPTER TWELVE

After that, evenings and especially nights at home were lonely. Sara continued to be depressed and to look at the negative side of everything. Despite recognizing that, she began to realize that she had been lonely for a while. She knew that her relationship with Peter had been falling apart, but the thought did not help defray her grief. She did not believe that things would not have been salvageable.

Over the next few months, Sara walked a lot with Bogey. It was the only thing that cheered her up at all. The exercise endorphins plus the exuberance of her lovable dog were enough to put a smile on her face. She had spent a lot of time with Bogey when he was a puppy and he was well trained to prance along at her side. He seemed to know she was hurting and tried extra hard to be good.

One evening when they were out walking, Sara had the distinct impression that she was being followed. Turning on her heel quickly in an effort to surprise, she saw a large man a half a block behind her. When he saw her turn, he quickly turned into a side street. It was disconcerting so she kept her guard up, but she didn't see him again. It nagged at her, though, because somehow he looked familiar.

That night, she realized where she had seen the man before. He had been at Peter's funeral – the one she had thought looked Italian and that she had felt unsettled about even then. She wondered who he was and what the hell he had to do with her. There was no good explanation, but there must be some reason that he had appeared in her life twice now. It couldn't be a coincidence.

She got out the registration book from the funeral and carefully went through the names. There were names that she did not recognize, but none of them looked particularly of Italian heritage. *Curious,* she thought, but she knew it didn't mean much. He might not have an ethnic name and for almost certain he would not have signed the registry.

That reminded her that she should start getting some thank you cards written – a long dreaded job. Sighing, she kept the book out, adding the flower list from the funeral home and another list of her own. First, she pulled up their Quicken software and took a close look at their finances. It had been a long time since she had looked at them, but she knew Peter kept a list of his passwords in the top drawer of his filing cabinet.

Everything seemed to be in order in the ledger. Luckily, Peter had been meticulous with financial details. She pulled the bank statements out of his file folder and it all balanced to the penny. She didn't even know exactly how much money he had made, but it was all here in black and white. He had been successful and had taken good care of her. It made her grateful to him on many levels. She wished she had paid more attention and had told him that in person.

People had often said, "One never knows how much time he/she has left on this earth". It had seemed cliché before, but now it was hitting home hard.

Each of the next four evenings, she worked on the notes. When all were finished, she set the envelopes on the kitchen table by her purse so she would not forget to post them in the morning. She was pouring fresh water for Bogey when the house phone rang. She set the dish down and answered it. "Hello!" she said. Then, "Hello!" a little louder. There was no answer, but clearly someone was listening.

"Hello?" Then there was a click in her ear and the line went dead. *Now this is spooky,* she thought. She hugged Bogey tightly, then put him on a leash and had him stay with her as she checked to make sure every window and door was locked. She set the house alarm and took Bogey with her to her upstairs bedroom.

After tossing and turning for several hours, she took a sleeping pill and soon drifted off into a much needed sound sleep.

CHAPTER THIRTEEN

Finally back in the office with the funeral and time behind her, Sara found piles of notes and files on her desk. Patsy had done the best she could to keep up and several others had pitched in, but there was still a lot to do. She knew she would be back to working late.

One day after sitting for four hours diligently working her way through the mess on her desk, she decided to get up and stretch her legs. Heading for the break room and a much anticipated cup of coffee, she passed Greg Smythe's door. Glancing inside, she saw Greg pulling Jen toward him and kissing her. She stopped and watched, shocked beyond belief. It was a long and lingering kiss. As soon as it ended, Sara quickly moved on, poured her coffee and sat down at a table. Her head was reeling. *What the hell? How was she going to talk Jen out of this?*

Just then, Jen walked in to get her own cup of coffee. "Hi, Aunt Sara," she chirped.

"Lord, Jen," she answered. "Is that all you have to say? I just saw Greg Smythe kissing you and it was a helluva kiss." She couldn't keep the anger out of her voice.

Jen immediately recoiled. “Are you spying on me?”

“Not at all. I was simply walking past the office on the way here. His door was wide open and there you were. It was a completely innocent observation. But now that I’ve seen it, what’s going on??

She went on, unable to contain herself. “Jen, he is fifteen years older than you are. Don’t you think he’s taking advantage of you? How could you participate in this? Do you think you love him?”

“No, not at all, Aunt Sara. It’s not like that. You wouldn’t understand.”

“Try me. Your mother would kill both of us if she knew!”

That made Jen laugh. “It’s really not like that at all. I’m trying to trick him.”

“You mean you’re leading him on?”

“Exactly.”

“Why?”

“Because he’s a dirt bag and I want to catch him.”

“What do you mean? He’s a good employee – doing a good job.”

“That’s what you think,” Jen said. “Actually there’s something going on. Here’s what I know so far. There is all kinds of cash in his desk. Big amounts of cash. And whenever he takes me out for drinks, we run into people and it’s like he has these clandestine conversations.”

“What kind of **DRINKS**?”

“Kool-Aid, Aunt Jen, what do you think? Hey, I’m 26 and I know not to over-drink. You don’t have to worry. Will you please just listen to me?”

“OK. But exactly **WHAT** do you mean by clandestine conversations?”

“When we run into people, he will excuse himself and go talk to them somewhere else – somewhere I can’t overhear the conversation. I watch out of the corner of my eye though and they are always looking around to be sure no one is watching. There’s always an exchange but I can’t see what it is. It’s small though, so I think it’s drugs. It’s definitely something illegal or why would he keep the money in cash and lock it in his drawer in the office?”

Sara interrupted. “For God’s sake, Jen. You’ve been watching too much TV. How can you be so naive?”

Then she doubted herself and added more thoughtfully, "How did you see the money?"

"The drawer was open one time when I went in. I didn't acknowledge that I'd seen it. He doesn't know."

Sara was adamant. "Thank God! You could be getting yourself into a dangerous situation! I forbid you to see him again!"

"Aunt Sara. Stop. I know you love me. I know you are worried about me, but I can handle myself. I know you don't want to believe it, but I'm an adult." She pronounced it a-DULT for emphasis.

Sara put her head in her hands. "Oh my God. Now I'm going to worry myself to death over you. Why me?"

"I'm sorry you found out this way. I meant to tell you, but you were so upset over Uncle Peter's death and had so much to do. It seemed unnecessary to burden you."

Jen was silent for a few minutes, and then said, "I would have told you eventually." She looked contrite.

Sara sighed. "Actually, this could explain a lot."

"What do you mean?" Jen asked, but Sara didn't answer.

Jen went on. “Here’s the real problem, though, and this it’s time you came to grips with it. I am now sure that Patsy is in love with Greg.”

Sara looked thoughtful. “That also would explain a lot.”

“What do you mean?” Jen asked.

“Well, like you said before. Patsy could be jealous of you. I’m guessing you are right that it’s the reason she accused you of stealing petty cash and said the other interns are jealous that you are getting special treatment. She could be talking them into that because she is mad about your supposed relationship with Greg. I’ve heard them arguing. I couldn’t make out what they were talking about, but they were clearly having a fight.”

“Should I talk with her?”

“No, not at this point. Let’s let this play out.” Sara thought a minute, and then said, “I think we have to call the police. They can hopefully set up a plan to catch Greg in the act and find out what the hell is going on.”

Jen answered immediately. “That’s fine with me. If you want to know the truth, I sort of feel like I’m in over my head.”

"I agree with you! You can't risk any more involvement in this – whatever it is. Everything you said to me is an indicator that he is doing something wrong. Please stay away from him!"

She could understand Jen's quest to catch Greg. She did come by it honestly. Jen was just like her mother. Stubborn as a mule. Like a dog with a bone when something seemed mysterious. She sipped her coffee as memories surfaced of her sister, Jen's mother, Corinne. They had both devoured every Nancy Drew book they could get their hands on. Sara had kept them all and passed them on to Jen on her twelfth birthday. It was a natural instinct to want to catch Greg. She wanted to herself.

Just then, Jake poked his head in the door and excitedly called to them. "Hey you two, come on out here! Take a look at the screen in the Pit." He could hardly contain himself. "They've got two more suspects for the City Centre bombing in custody!"

Jen looked sheepish and followed as Sara jumped up and led the way out the door.

Whenever there were extraordinary news breaks, everyone left their offices and gathered in the central Pit in front of the big screen TV. It was affectionately called "the Pit" because the floor of the circular area was about four feet lower than the floor of the office area above it. There were four staircases leading into it – equidistant from each other, so there was one at each end and one at each side of the circle. Offices were grouped around the sides of the upper level, each with a large window to the outside. Desks were grouped in the middle of the Pit, with files and work areas arranged around its curved sides. Because of their constant proximity, those that worked in this area – compliance officers and a few assistants - were the closest to each other of all the employees.

The TV was above the stairs on the east side and the channel was tuned to CNN. On the screen were indeed two current mug shots next to the original police drawings of the two male suspects. The resemblance was clear. The witnesses had done a good job of describing the men.

“Where did they find them? How did they get them?” Sara asked.

Jake had an incredulous tone of voice as he answered the question. “You won’t believe it. They guys are idiots. One would think they would try to get as far away as possible, but the jerks went into the Cheers Bar! Luckily this amazing waitress recognized them when she took their order and she kept her cool! Look, there she is. She’s telling it again now.”

They listened as waitress Norma Salyer's face filled the screen. She was a pretty girl, probably in her twenties, with a bouncy, short pony tail. She was wearing a black, close fitting, low cut dress and a white pinafore type apron. She chewed gum as she explained that the two men had come in and been seated in her section. She had seen the police drawings of the suspects and recognized them immediately.

"I couldn't believe they were TOGETHAH," she said in her thick Bostonian accent. "I knew it was them," she said again. Cool as cucumbers, they both ordered giant Norm burgers and cheesy fries. Maybe I'm imaginin' it, but they looked, like, triumphant or somethin' or like they was celebratin' somethin'. Like they had cat shit grins on their faces. Know what I mean? They thought they was somethin' for sure. Right there in plain sight!"

"So what did you do next? The reporter asked.

"Well, it was all I could do to contain myself, so I just chewed my gum real hard and tried to stay calm. I went over and put their order in, then took another one and put it in before I ducked into the kitchen. I made sure they wasn't lookin' first though. Know what I mean?"

"Yes I do," the reporter chuckled. "And then what?"

"I went out the back door of the kitchen where nobody could hear me and I dialed 911 on my cell phone which I always keep in my pocket right here." She pulled it out and showed the reporter. "And I told the police the whole story and I told them where the guys was sittin' in the middle of the restaurant, not by the windows. I didn't want nobody to get alerted and I didn't want them to get away and I didn't want nobody to get scared and give it away. So then I put my phone back and then I went back out into the restaurant and minded my own business. I gave them guys water and said it would be about ten minutes on the burgers because we cook them all fresh and they're thick – just like I always say and they said OK."

She went on excitedly. "Next thing I knew, four police walked through the door and straight to the table I had told 'em about. They called out the guy's names, told 'em to stand up and handcuffed 'em. Right there. Right in our Cheers Bar! Can you believe it? They checked 'em for guns and they didn't even have any!" She laughed. "They just thought they were gonna go out and get a Norm burger like everybody else." She shook her head.

The reporter grinned and everybody in the Pit cheered.

Sara was beside herself. "Look at that! They don't look very remorseful." She was mad. "Murderers" she said. "Nothing but murderers. I'm glad they didn't get their Norm burgers because they don't deserve them."

Jake looked at her and raised his eyebrows. When she looked back, she realized the humor in the situation.

"Don't make me laugh, Jake. It's not funny."

"Yes, it is, Sara" he said softly. "And it's cause for celebration! They got them! Hopefully soon we'll have some answers about WHY this happened."

"It really is weird, though," he went on. "How often do suspects get captured that easily? They didn't even put up a fight. They were so sure of themselves they didn't even hide! Just like the women.

"Yes, I know. I certainly hope we'll get some answers soon. The suspense is killing me. You know, it's funny. I thought the drawings looked like the bombers were Middle Eastern, but now I think my mind was just playing with me. In person, they don't look that at all and the women certainly weren't. It will be really interesting to see what their reasons were for his senseless bombing."

She kept staring at the screen, listening for more details and didn't notice Jen slinking out the door.

That night, in bed she tossed and turned, torn between feelings of concern that Jen would do something stupid and imagining every possible way she could take Greg down. She needed to find proof of illegal activity. But of course the whole thing was preposterous. Greg was a grown man and she would have no chance against him. She could not possibly let on that she had any suspicions.

CHAPTER FOURTEEN

It was just a few days later that they had answers about the bombing. The attackers gave up information quickly. The next news flash announced that the building bombing was not a terrorist act at all. The men who were captured belonged to a national activist group that was against abortion. One man was Mexican and one was Brazilian. There was an abortion clinic in the building on the fifth floor – practically right in the middle. The easiest way to bomb it – or rather, to be sure to destroy it - was to take the whole building down – and why not do that to increase attention anyway.

It was mortifying for Sara to think about. All of the innocent lives lost that had nothing to do with the clinic – not to mention those that did. The whole thing was shocking. She had known there were medical offices in the building but it had never occurred to her that there was any threat associated with them.

Jake had stopped by when he heard the news. He had a sad look on his face. "Well, at least it gives us some closure," he said.

"Yes, but it's not much of a comfort. Is it?" He shook his head and she went on.

"The funny thing is… I was so convinced it was Middle Eastern terrorists and then this comes out. It just goes to show you that a person shouldn't jump to conclusions. You really never know until you have proof. I'll certainly try not to do that in the future."

"Well, that's easy to say but hard to do. Good luck!" He laughed. "Hopefully they'll find the other two. Unfortunately I don't think any of us are very safe either way."

"Yeah. I'm sure you're right." She hesitated, and then said, "Jake, on a very different subject, have you heard any rumors about Greg and Patsy?"

"No, why?"

"Oh, I don't know. Some things just seem funny. I've heard some things. I was wondering if they were – you know – together."

"Really? I haven't heard or seen a thing. But then, I'm sure I would be the last to know. People tend to try to keep things like that from me because there would be consequences. If you think there's something, though, I'll keep my eye out. I suppose it's not out of the question" he mused. "He's a pretty charming guy. I hope not though because I certainly have been pleased with the revenue he's bringing in!"

"Yes, he's doing well. Unbelievably well. But OK. It's probably nothing. I could be imagining it."

"Don't worry about it. I'll look into it. See you later!"

She waved as he went out her office door.

However, over the next few weeks, issues in the office worsened. Sara overheard snippets of other staff conversations about Greg and Patsy. Their relationship was clearly becoming known. She also saw in-fighting and jealousy because Greg was so successful. His stock trades were large and lucrative. It was impossible to ignore the fact that his business was growing quickly – too quickly – impossibly quickly. It was drawing everyone's attention.

Sara had noticed an astonished look on Chuck's face the day before when he was reviewing some paperwork and she was still curious about it. She was having a conversation with John on the other side of the room when Greg came sauntering in. He had a stock order in his hand. She had noticed how trim he was as he bent over to say something quietly into Chuck's ear as he dropped the paper on his desk. She wondered what the secrecy was about.

Standing beside her, John followed her gaze. "Nice looking guy, huh," he said mockingly.

She looked up surprised at the tone of his voice. *What must he be thinking?* she wondered. She drew herself up straight and gave him a carefully constructed reply. "Yes, of course. You can see that for yourself. But there's a lot of that around." She said snippily and then turned and walked away.

Sara's suspicion of Greg continued to grow. One evening, she worked until almost 9 pm, deliberately planning to stay until everyone had left. When she could hear no more sounds, she walked to her office door and looked out. All the lights were off and everyone appeared to be gone. Still, she walked down the hall, looking into each office to be sure. The offices were set up in a circle – all with outside windows, with break and storage rooms in the areas without windows. The circular area was in the middle. The floor was marble and ergonomic chairs stuffed and covered with red, patterned fabric graced every desk. She flipped on a few peripheral lights, went down into the Pit. She made a circle, looking into every office and listening for sounds to be sure there was no one around.

Her heart was pounding as she headed for Greg's office door. She had to find some evidence – something to incriminate him. She knew there was something going on, but what?

Entering his office, Sara left the door open so she could hear anyone who might approach. She could see without turning on a light because it was an outside office with lots of windows. There was plenty of light coming in from the outdoor building lights. First, she checked the drawer Jen had talked about and as she expected, it was locked. Opening his desk, she searched for keys, but didn't find any. Opening other drawers, she looked through them without seeing anything suspicious.

Next, she looked through Greg's filing cabinet. Nothing suspicious there either – just a rather messy collection of client files, not even in alphabetical order. It was then that she heard the footsteps. *Oh my God. I have no reason to be in here! What will I say?* She looked around for a place to hide and jumped into a thin coat closet, carefully closing the door as quietly as she could. She put her ear against the door and heard Greg come in the office. She knew it was him because he was almost always whistling. It usually drove her crazy, but at this moment she was grateful. She continued to listen, trying not to breathe or to make any noise. She thanked her lucky stars that there were only hooks and not any noisy hangers she could bump into.

Greg was walking around. She heard a drawer open and close. Then she heard him leave and close the door. *He must have forgotten something,* she thought. Sara waited in the closet for a good five minutes after he left and then carefully cracked the door to peek out. She tiptoed over to the office door and looked out. He had switched off all of the peripheral lights he had flipped on but there was not a sound to be heard.

She turned back toward the desk and noticed a book on the credenza that hadn't been there before. Quickly, she walked over and opened it. It wasn't a book at all. It was a ledger with cash entries that started about a year before – just about the time that Greg had started at Jordon and Associates. She recognized a few of the names because they were Presidents and CEOs of major companies. Payments were listed by each name – each just under $10,000. She knew the reason for that. Payments of $10,000 or more had to be reported to the IRS. *Was Greg laundering money?*

Sara turned page after page of entries amounting to several million dollars. The next section showed the same type of payments flowing back in the other direction to the same people. Toward the back of the book were lists of stock transactions. There were a number of large purchases showing huge profits at sale. She was quite sure that in at least a couple of cases, the names of either the CEO or President of the company whose stock had been purchased were in the book. They were buying each other's stocks in groups.

Her mind was reeling. *It must be insider trading! What an idiot he was to have documented this all manually! Having this all in one place clearly tied it all together.*

If she was right, this book contained more than enough proof. It certainly contained damning evidence of something. She had to check it out, but she couldn't steal the book. Greg would miss it. He must have inadvertently left it here. It wasn't the sort of thing anyone would leave out in the open on purpose. Maybe he would be back to get it!

Sara closed the book and made a beeline for the copy room. Switching the machine on, she tried to calm herself as it hummed to life. She placed the book face down on the screen and chose legal sized paper so she could copy two pages at a time. It still took twenty nerve wracking minutes to get the job done. Finally, she had the pile of papers she wanted and was able to switch off the machine. She literally ran back to Greg's office and replaced the journal on the credenza. Leaving the office, she closed the door as he had done and headed back toward her office, picking up the stack of papers in the copy room on the way. She had just finished stuffing them into her briefcase when the hall light popped on. *Oh my God. Someone's here!*

She sat down at her desk. Luckily she hadn't turned off her computer, so she swung around and quickly pulled up a client file to appear to be working. A few minutes later, Greg was standing in her doorway saying, "Hey, you're working late! Or did you just get here? I was just here and it didn't seem like anyone was around." Her hands were shaking so she put them in her lap as she turned toward the door.

"Yep, I'm here," she said, her face frozen like a deer in headlights. "Just catching up on a few things. You know, not much to go home for these days. Bogey is taken care of and it tends to be a bit lonely."

"I suppose not," he replied. "Maybe we should have dinner some time?"

Sara's stomach turned over, but she didn't let on. "Maybe" she said, as coquettishly as she could under the circumstances.

"Yeah. Maybe. Don't work yourself to death, Sara. A girl should have a little fun." He smiled.

She tried to smile back. "I know. I'm almost done. I won't be much longer."

"OK. See you tomorrow." He waved the ledger at her and turned to leave.

"See you tomorrow."

Greg felt unsettled as he walked away down the hall. He couldn't put his finger on it, but something didn't feel right. Sara seemed on edge. Could she possibly know anything? He had been so careful. That had to be pretty impossible. Maybe he had better move up his exit plan.

When she was sure Greg had left the building, Sara quickly shut down her computer and put it in her briefcase, switched off her office lights and headed for the parking garage. She felt edgy, like a person must feel when they're walking through Customs with contraband. She wanted to get this stuff out of here and hidden away as fast as she could.

CHAPTER FIFTEEN

On the way home that night, Sara was overcome by fear. Her mind was flashing back to 1997 when she had inadvertently uncovered an investment scam and things got pretty hairy before all was said and done. Her life had been threatened and since then she always kept her head up. She kept looking in her rear view mirror to try to be sure she was not being followed. She was so happy to pull into her garage. She turned off the ignition and sat in the locked car until the door was safely down.

Only then did she get out and enter the house. In the house, she greeted Bogey and then warily checked every room. It was irrational because Bogey was large and he was a great watch dog. She couldn't imagine that anyone would try to come in with him roaming around. She left him in his run on nice mornings and Katie would come to feed him and put him in the house when she was working late. Thank goodness because she did not want to go back out to get him out of his run.

She looked in the fridge for something to eat, but was more curious than hungry. Besides, she didn't want to take the time to cook. Instead she opened a bottle of wine, poured a glass and then grabbed a box of wheat thins and a tub of pimento cheese.

She took her drink and snack into her office with her briefcase. She could not wait to get a better look at the sheaf of papers. While her computer was booting up, she spread them out on her desk.

It was pretty easy to find out who belonged to the names on the sheet simply by googling them. They were all prominent people – rich people, with histories. As she had guessed, many were Presidents or CEO's of companies. As she discovered who they were, she wrote the information next to each name. Then came the shock. There were thirty names in all and one of them was Peter's. Peter Jensen. There is was, as big as life.

The payments next to Peter's name alone totaled six hundred thousand dollars. *What? Where did this money come from?* She flipped to the back of the book where she knew she would find the payments and Peter's returns totaled over three million dollars. Sara snorted. *There certainly isn't three million dollars in our account!*

She knew she could get to the bottom of this because bank routing numbers and account numbers were written beside the payments. It was only a matter of time. She would call Henry Moses in the morning. He was originally a friend's attorney, but she had had him do some work for her also and in the process they had become friends.

Henry would be the perfect sleuth. He was a tiny, wiry man and his big, round, black glasses made him look more like a bookworm than a powerful attorney. But what he lacked in physical presence, he made up for in unsurpassed knowledge and ability to get the impossible done. No one had contacts like Henry. He would be able to track this down anywhere in the world.

Now Sara was starting to get angry. She wanted to know the truth and she wanted to know it NOW. But first, she needed a little more information. She finished googling the list of names to identify the people involved and then started googling the companies. In many cases, she found expansive company events like mergers, acquisitions, announcements that would surely push the stock higher. She wrote these by each company name with the dates they occurred. Then she compared the dates with the stock purchases in those companies. In every case, the purchases had been made a month to six weeks before the event. It was a clear case of insider trading.

It was two a.m. before Sara finished her project. She tried to sleep, but too many thoughts were rolling around in her head. *How did Peter get involved in this? Why did he get involved? Where is the money? How does he know Greg?* The whole thing was completely unsettling.

CHAPTER SIXTEEN

Sara finally fell asleep at 5 a.m. and woke up three hours later. She immediately picked up her mobile phone and dialed Henry Moses. She knew he always arrived at the office early because he liked to leave early and play golf. Sure enough, he answered the phone. When Sara swore him to secrecy and told him her story he was incredulous. She gave him the routing and account numbers written by Peter's name and asked him if he could use his contacts to find out where the account was and what its status was. Maybe that would help her figure out a piece to the puzzle. He said he understood the urgency and would get back as soon as possible. She hung up the phone feeling anxious. There was no way she could go into the office this morning and risk running into Greg.

Her next call was to Jake. Not only the owner of the company she worked for, he had also become a friend. He didn't have a named office manager, but she had been there so long that he often came to her to discuss office issues. She trusted him completely and found herself turning to him more and more. She told him about the problems with Patsy and Jen. Then she told him about the ledger book and her concerns. She told him she had made a copy of it and had it at home.

Jake had his headset on and was walking around his office wringing his hands. He was worried and concerned, both from a personal and a professional standpoint. "How do you think we should proceed?" he asked. "Shall I call the police?"

"Give me just a little more time," she replied. "I'm not sure we can prove anything yet." Then she told him about Peter's name being in the ledger and her call to Henry Moses.

"Holy Christ, Sara. What next! How can that be possible? Please tell me you didn't know anything at all about it. You didn't, right?"

"No, of course not, Jake. You know me better than that. Let's see what Henry finds out. I'm sure it won't take him long."

"OK, but you only have overnight, do you hear me? This is my firm and if there's fraud going on, I want to get an investigator on it as soon as possible. We have to limit the damage. It's risky to wait."

"Got it. I'll call you as soon as I hear."

They both hung up their phones with worried looks on their faces.

Several hours later, she was pacing around her house with Bogey following her from room to room when her phone rang. It had seemed like an eternity.

"Hi Sara. Henry Moses here. Are you sitting down?"

"No, but I can be. Why?"

She sat down as he said, "I called in a favor and found out information about the account. It was a big favor because it's in a country that normally doesn't give out information – Switzerland. And this is why I asked you to sit down. It contains three and a half million dollars. Not only that, here's the real kicker. The account has been accessed since Peter's death."

"What? she cried. "How can that be possible? It must be Greg! Or someone else has access to that account!"

"It's not Greg, but there are two signers so it must be the partner since it couldn't't' be Peter. My contact faxed me the signature card. Peter's signature is clear but the other one isn't. All I can make out is Gui in the first name and a capital B with a scrawl in the last name. It's virtually unreadable."

"Can you find out through the bank?"

"That's not as easy as it sounds. Like I said, they don't give out personal information. It's nearly impossible, but I'll do what I can. I can't guarantee I can find out."

"But I'm Peter's heir so it's my money now!" she cried out.

"Sara, calm down. It's in another country and you are not a signer. Good luck with that! Besides, there are several things you perhaps have not considered." He lowered his head and looked over his glasses at her.

"First of all, this money was obtained illegally. Correct?"

She nodded. "I think so, but now that you mention it, how can I be sure?"

"I don't know. But the fact that this money was directly wired out of the country makes me suspect there was some tax evasion, correct?"

She nodded her head miserably. "I guess so."

"It will clearly take the IRS and the SEC a while to figure out what to do with it, but believe me this money is not coming to you."

"I see your point," she said, and went on, speaking in a monotone.

“OK then. Thanks, Henry. I appreciate it. It’s just so unbelievable. I really can’t wrap my head around this at all. Please just try and keep me out of this the best you can.”

“I don’t think you have to worry about that since you can testify honestly that you knew nothing about it and you have not signed anything. This is all in Peter’s lap and whatever partners he had. As long as you don’t touch any money or sign anything, you should be all right.”

“You are in shock,” he went on. “Give it some time. These things usually sort themselves out eventually. Someone will make a mistake and the whole thing will come out. In the meantime though, you had better talk to the authorities in order to make your position clear.”

“Yes, I know you’re right. I know just who to call. I have a friend with the SEC who will know what to do. Bye, Henry and thanks again.”

“Bye, Sara. Keep your chin up!”

Her next call was again to Jake, who immediately called Maureen Sommerfield, an SEC investigator that they both knew well and had worked with before. He kept Sara on the phone as he dialed and then conferenced her in. Luckily Maureen was in her office and picked up the phone. After exchanging niceties, Jake asked Sara to tell her the whole story and she launched in.

“Whoa. Just a second,” Maureen said. “Let me get my headset on and open a WORD document. I need to take notes.

They waited a couple of minutes until she said, “OK, shoot. Start over please.” Sara started again, speaking slowly and deliberately, trying to keep the story to the facts before she offered her own conclusions. Several times, Maureen stopped her to ask questions. They could hear the keyboard keys clicking as she took copious notes.

When they had finished, Maureen confirmed that they had a case worth investigating. She cautioned them to keep the story to themselves and to do nothing suspicious that might alert Greg. It was absolutely crucial that he continue as if nothing had happened so that he didn’t try and run.

CHAPTER SEVENTEEN

Driving home a few evenings later, Sara turned down the street before her own. She wanted to stop and leave an envelope in the milk box on the side of Katie's house. It contained a check made out to her for taking care of Bogey over the past few weeks. The street was arched with old elm trees and filled with beautiful Tudor style homes. Katie lived with her parents who had been there since 1952. Not much had changed since then and Sara always admired that. Each house still had a little door by the larger side door where once upon a time milk in glass bottles had been delivered by the local dairy.

She got out of her car and as she walked toward the box, she glanced through the gap to her street where she could see her own house. She did a double-take. *Oh no. There's a light on! Who could be there?* Placing the envelope in the box, she turned and jumped back in her car to hurry home. When she rounded the corner to enter her own street, she again looked at her house. No light. *What?* She thought. *Was I imagining things? I must have been. I never leave lights on. I'm really good about that.*

She hit the garage door button to open it and parked her car in the garage, hitting the button again to close the door. Getting out, she had an overwhelming feeling of dread. Shaking it off, she went inside. As she took her coat off, she shivered. There was a draft coming from the window over the kitchen sink. Looking at it more closely, she discovered it was slightly ajar. As she shoved it shut and twisted the lock, she realized the alarm had not gone off. She had been too preoccupied to notice immediately.

And what about Bogey? Where is Bogey? He always bounded to the door to greet her. She went back outside to check his run but he wasn't there. This gave her an additional signal of alarm. Re-entering the house, she announced her arrival with a lot of noise, hoping to scare off anyone who might be there. Then she heard Bogey whimpering. But from where? She called out his name and Bogey started barking, clearly from behind the laundry room door. *She froze. Oh my God. Did I lock him in there this morning when I left? How could I? There's no water in there!*

Coming to her senses, she rushed to open the door to save the dog, who jumped up and covered her face with kisses. As she was hugging him, she noticed a piece of a gnawed steak bone on the floor of the laundry room. Now she knew something was up. She never gave Bogey bones. Someone must have lured him in there and slammed the door. She gave him a drink of water, attached his leash which was always hanging by the back door and took him out. She walked all around the house with the dog looking for signs of life or a break-in but found nothing. She wondered, *is it possible that someone entered with a key? How could that be?* Only Katie and Jen had keys and they would never lock Bogey up.

Before re-entering, she took her mobile phone out of her pocket and dialed 911. The police station was just around the corner and two officers arrived within minutes. The officers drew their guns. She kept Bogey beside her on the leash and followed them through the house. They started in the basement and found nothing amiss. On the first floor everything also seemed to be in its place. They opened every closet door to make sure no one was in there hiding.

Then they headed upstairs. Things looked in order – even the piles of Peter's things that she and Jen had sorted and left on the landing to be taken to Good Will. Entering her bedroom, it appeared the same, until they came to the closet. The large walk-in closet had two sides, one that was hers and one that had been Peter's. In Peter's, not much was left – just a few things that she couldn't bear to part with. The most important thing was missing.

"Wait a minute," she gasped. There was a beautiful wooden box here on this shelf. It's gone.

"And what was in it?" Officer Peyton asked.

"An old and very expensive watch. Baum and Mercier. I gave it to Peter on our wedding day. I know he kept it in there. Some old keys. I don't know what they unlocked."

She paused, trying to remember.

"Some cash, but not enough to break in a house for, and I don't know what else. I didn't pay much attention. I kept the box because I also gave that to him as an anniversary present and the watch was always in there when he wasn't wearing it."

"And that's all that's missing?"

"Yes, best I can tell."

"Weird," said Officer Maxman.

"Well, I guess that's good. And clearly no one is in the house so I think you're good to go now. We'll just dust this shelf for fingerprints and take a look outside and see if we see anything."

"I already did that."

"I know, but you might have missed something. You never know."

They found a partial fingerprint on the shelf and did indeed find something she missed – but inside the house not outside. The alarm wire had been pulled out of the box by the kitchen door. That's why it had malfunctioned."

"Funny that it didn't send a signal to the station. Doesn't it usually?

"Yes, it does."

"Hmmm. I can re-attach this so it will work tonight, but you had better get the alarm company out to check out the broken wire option, OK?"

"Sure, I'll do that right away," she said, perplexed.

"OK then. We'll get back to you about this fingerprint. Hopefully it's enough to find out who was in here."

"Thanks," she said gratefully.

When they left, she took another look at all of the windows and doors and made sure they were locked. Then she called Jen and asked her if they could meet for breakfast the next morning at The Bristol in the Four Seasons Hotel. She knew that was an offer Jen couldn't refuse and there were some things she wanted to talk about.

Again, Sara slept fitfully that night. The break-in had been unnerving.

CHAPTER EIGHTEEN

The pervasive smell of bacon was in the air as Sara approached the restaurant. Her mind was on Jen. Maybe it was time to seize Jen's comment about not wanting to be an investment advisor and encourage her to find a different job. She didn't like what Jen was getting herself into. Even though she didn't know the specific details, whatever it was couldn't be good. She certainly didn't like what she thought could be going on with Greg and she didn't want to risk anything bad happening to her only niece.

She was seated at their table when Jen walked through the door. Jen loved The Bristol and was dressed to the nines. Her high heels clicked along the floor as she hurried over.

"Hey, Aunt Sara. What's the occasion?" She leaned down and gave her aunt an affectionate hug.

Sara smiled. "Nothing at all. Things have been hectic lately and I just wanted to spoil my favorite niece."

"Your **ONLY** niece," Jen laughed.

"Well, whatever." She smiled. "Still favorite. Are you going to get your usual?"

"You bet!"

"Well then, so am I." Her grin was infectious.

The waiter approached with two glasses of champagne, which they accepted, clicked together and sipped. He had two menus tucked under his arm, which he proceeded to offer, but they waved him away.

"I think we know what we want," Sara said. "Go ahead, Jen."

"Two short stacks of lemon ricotta hotcakes, two bowls of maple and pecan granola, two sparkling waters and two cups of coffee - black."

The waiter laughed. "Here are a couple of ladies who know what they like!" He left humming and they smiled at each other.

After exchanging a few pleasantries, Sara broached the subject that was on her mind.

"So you don't want to be an investment advisor. You told me that. So what would you like to do? Maybe it's time you moved on."

"So that's what this is all about. Do you want me out of the office? Wait a minute. Are you *FIRING* me?"

"Not at all, Jen. You said that on your own. Don't you remember? I'm just trying to make sure you're happy. As much as I like having you work for Jordon and Associates, I want to keep your best interests in mind."

"Oh, I see," Jen said, pouting. "Well, I'm not ready to leave yet, so please don't make me go, but I don't think it's something I want to do long term."

"I see." Sara waited to see what Jen would say next.

"I don't know what I want to do – but certainly something meaningful. Maybe something that will help people?"

Sara laughed. "You and every other twenty something. It was the same in my day. That's an easy thing to say when you have no clue what you want to do. Is that it?"

She went on. "You know, Jen. It simply takes a while – for most people at least – to figure their lives out. And besides that, it's an ever changing ball game. What makes you happy may change over time."

The look on Jen's face was disturbed, but she was listening and looking intently at her aunt.

“Here’s my advice, Jen. Over the next two weeks, think about what you are doing when you are smiling. Don’t force it. Just let it happen, but recognize it when it happens. Honey, you have the luxury of doing whatever you want to do and you should be thrilled about that because not everyone does. On the other hand, it’s almost a curse because the field is wide open. Just remember that no one is going to decide for you.”

“I like marketing.” The thought immediately burst out.

“That’s good because that was your major in college, but what do you specifically mean by that? Marketing is a broad word and encompasses a lot of things. That’s not specific enough. Do you like social networking? Do you like graphic arts? Advertising? Being a client rep? See what I mean?”

“I think I do. There are lots of things I like but there are also lots of things I don’t like. Most of the things I don’t like involve people I don’t like.

Sara laughed. “Unfortunately you’re going to have to get used to that because people are everywhere – especially in marketing. You always have to please the people.”

“And that’s not all,” Sara said. “Think about the word meaningful itself. Not right now, but work on defining what that means to you. Emphasis on **TO**

YOU. When you really think about meaningful, I think you'll realize that it has more to do with yourself than with others. No one else is going to make you happy. All of us girls grow up thinking that, but take it from me, it's not true. There are no knights in shining armor or completely fulfilling jobs out there. They may seem so at first, but where the rubber meets the road, you have to always be standing on your own two feet to be happy. There's no way around it. You're going to get clobbered in life and you have to be strong and ready for it."

"THAT'S encouraging," Jen giggled.

"I think you know what I mean." Sara smiled.

"Yes, I think I do. Let me give this some thought and I'll get back to you, OK? For the moment, let's just enjoy this fabulous breakfast."

"Deal."

CHAPTER NINETEEN

When Sara went to the office, she tried to act like nothing had happened – either at work or at home. In reality, she was as nervous as a hen who knew there was a fox in the chicken coop. It was difficult to work, wondering about the bizarre break-in as well as what the SEC was doing in the background to catch Greg in the act. Maureen deliberately left her out of the loop so she could not be implicated. She didn't really want to know anyway. God forbid that she would accidentally give something away! She knew the police would have to be involved somehow and wondered if Moe would have a part in it. After all, she had met him when Maureen had hired him to protect her when she had gotten herself into another foul situation a few years before. He had close ties to the SEC and they trusted him.

Several days later, Sara was in the Pit looking for a file. It was near five pm and fairly quiet. Voices carried across the room. John Banfield and Chuck Pentley were talking to each other. Sara's ears perked up when she heard Greg's name.

"Wow, I don't know how Greg does it," John said, shaking his head.

"I know! It's amazing how he finds all of these God-awful rich investors. I've never seen anything like it and I've been in this business a long time." Chuck shook his head too.

"I can't believe he has another one coming in tomorrow. John whistled. So this guy is bringing in two mill and as usual they'll tell us what to put it in. Not a bad order!"

"Yeah, it's a little weird though. Don't you think? Everybody else is **ASKING** us what to buy and Greg is **TELLING** us what to buy. And he has this uncanny knack for picking things that sky rocket sooner rather than later. The guy is a fortune teller!" Chuck exclaimed.

Grinning, John replied, "Whatever. I don't care how he does it, just as long as he does it. We're all making money on him. I'm sure the boss is head over heels!"

How can anyone be so stupid? Sara thought. Had these guys **KNOWN** this was going on and didn't bother to investigate it? Hadn't put two and two together because they were so happy to be making so much money? *Money is so blinding,* she thought. *It never changes.*

John and Chuck lowered their voices and she didn't hear the rest of the conversation.

Chuck tried to appear nonchalant as he asked John to do him a favor. “Here’s a list of numbers,” he said. “Would you please go look up the names associated with these accounts and make a list?”

“Sure, Buddy. But why?”

“I’ll show you why when you have the list.”

Thirty minutes later, John was back with the completed list – a name beside each number. He whistled and said, “Wow, there are some heavy hitters on here. I recognize almost all of these names. They’re CEOs of major companies all across the US. And did you notice the name of Peter Tannenhill? Could that possibly be Sara’s husband? Do you think she knows about this? What’s going on?”

“I’ll tell you soon. But first you have to do me another favor.”

John rolled his eyes. “All right, what?”

“Now take this other list of numbers and do the same thing.”

“OK,” he said resignedly. “I can’t wait to hear what you’ve got up your sleeve.”

In fifteen minutes, he was back with the second list and two cups of coffee. He handed a cup to Chuck, which was gratefully accepted. He set the list down and said, “Here you go.”

Chuck pulled a stack of papers out of his desk drawer. The top two were the same lists he had given to John. He proceeded to compare John’s answers to his own. John was looking over his shoulder. “Look. See here? They’re identical.”

“You sound surprised.”

“No, I’m not surprised at all. I just wanted to be sure I hadn’t made a mistake.”

“No mistakes that I can see.”

“So this is evidence, John. The names are the same as far back as I looked.”

“Which is how far?”

“9 months. These guys are trading as a pack. And what’s even more interesting is this graph. Here I look at the trades they made in terms of profit. The profit numbers are huge, but every so often they purposely – or so it seems – take a minor loss so they fly under the radar. Because it’s not complete profit, the computer doesn’t flag them.”

“Yikes.” John looked worried. “Do you think they’re insider trading?”

"I think that's pretty obvious, don't you? And here's the proof." Chuck pulled out another piece of paper that tracked major corporate announcements against the trades. In the case of the profits, buys had been made between four and six months before these announcements – again to stay under the radar. Because they were so far in advance, the buys had seemed like normal trades.

"I can't believe they've been getting away with this for so long. Do you think you should tell Jake?"

"I don't think I have any choice. You find out something like this and you don't report it and you could be deemed an accomplice. Geez. The firm has been executing these trades for them. We should have figured this out a long time ago. I feel like an idiot."

"So you're comfortable with being a whistle blower?"

"No, but I'm proud of it. I'll talk to Jake as soon as he comes in. Who knows. He may know something already. I've got to get to him as soon as I can."

"In the meantime, what shall we do?"

"Just keep on keeping on, John. We can't draw attention to this. Who knows what could happen. These are heavy hitters and if I'm honest I have to say I'm a little frightened by it all."

"Aw, you've been watching too many detective shows." John laughed.

"Touché," Chuck said, giving John a salute.

Just then, Jake walked in.

"Speak of the devil," John chortled.

"That's OK actually. I would like to get this over with." Chuck picked up his stack of papers and headed straight over to Jake, asking if they could please go into his office to talk.

Jake creased his eyebrows. He could tell that Chuck was upset about something. "Sure. Of course," he said immediately. "Let's go." There was never any time to waste when a compliance problem was unearthed.

Once tucked away from the prying ears and funny little echoes always to be found in the Pit, Chuck went through the whole scenario again, just as he had done with John, making a point to mention Sara's husband's involvement.

Jake put his reading glasses on and leaned his fist on his chin as he went through everything carefully. This was a serious allegation, but combined with the ledger book he already knew about, this list of proof of trades and their timing appeared to be the final proof that would tie this case together in a neat little bow. It would put Greg and his cohorts behind bars for a long time.

When he spoke, first he said, “Clever. Very clever. In fact, this scam is brilliant. As you noticed, the trades are carefully executed to keep the group under the radar. It looks like they bought into each other’s firms at significant times, but not their own so they didn’t need normal SEC approvals. Do you have copies of all of this, Chuck?”

“No, but I can go and make them if you like.”

“Please get a copy to me as quickly as you can. We must act immediately to sort this out. And by the way, good work! You have uncovered an incredible scheme that could bankrupt me – not to mention imply complicity - if I don’t act quickly. Thank you for coming to me the minute you discovered this.”

“Hey, no problem, boss. I don’t want to lose my job either.” He smiled half-heartedly and left the room with a worried look on his face.

When a copy of the stack was in his possession, he tucked it in his briefcase and went to talk to Sara.

CHAPTER TWENTY

Sara was sitting at her desk hard at work when Jake came to her office door. He stood a minute and watched her. She was slim and pretty, but always so intense. Engaging but a bit aloof. He knocked on the door and sent her one of his radiant smiles.

She was especially happy to see him when he told her why he had come. He noticed how she lit up and showed her Chuck's findings, running through the detail and telling her his thoughts. When she thought he had finished, he stood up and looked at her in a knowing way. She noticed there was one more piece of paper in his hand.

"That's not all, is it? she asked.

"No. I've saved the best for last."

"There's **MORE**?"

"Yes, there's more." He sighed. "I can't believe this, but when I started to suspect there were some shall we say 'issues' with Greg, I had him investigated. He has a record."

"I guess you don't mean the old fashioned vinyl kind," she quipped.

He smiled but didn't laugh. "No, I don't. Greg has been in prison!"

She leaned her head on her hand. "Seriously?"

"Yes, seriously. I'm so embarrassed about how I found this out. Look at this." He laid the last piece of paper on her desk. It was a copy of an Internet article about industry fraud that focused on criminals in the business, written by a very knowledgeable blogger.

"A blogger? Oh my God. A **BLOGGER** exposed this? And by the way, how did he get past the firm's security check?"

"I can't find a security check in the files. There must have been some collusion somehow. Jerry Jones was in charge of that. Remember him? Greg came just about the time he left the firm. Somehow Greg must have slipped through the cracks."

"What was he in prison for?"

"Drugs and insurance fraud." Jake looked heartsick. "I can't believe this got past me. I have to prosecute him and then figure out some way to explain this to my firm's investors. There's no excuse. When it all comes out, I'm going to have to own up to my mistake. I just hope we can survive this."

“Oh Jake. I’m so sorry.” And she truly meant it.

Then she pulled out the information she had taken from Greg’s office and went through it with Jake. They matched the money coming in to the trading records, which of course fed together perfectly.

Jake asked her to call Maureen to tell her he was on his way with the information, which she did immediately. Maureen picked up the phone on the second ring. She was in the office and although she was about to leave, she said she would gladly wait.

A couple more days went by with nothing out of the ordinary occurring. Sara knew she had to stop reading something into everything she saw or she was going to go crazy. The secret about Greg and his shenanigans was eating her alive.

She did, at least, finally have a chance to get Patsy alone. It wasn’t an easy conversation.

“Hi Patsy,” she said as calmly as she could. “I talked to Jen and I really don’t think she has anything to do with the petty cash situation. I also really don’t think she is getting any special favors. You have to admit she’s good at what she does and she should be rewarded for that, don’t you think?”

Patsy looked at her incredulously. "Do you seriously doubt my word? After all the time we've been together, this really hurts."

"Please don't put it that way. You know Jen almost as well as I do. She is as honest as the day is long. It's hard for me to understand why you would doubt her."

"Because. Just because. I don't know why. I just don't like the way she has grown up and I don't trust her. You just can't see it because of the family relationship." She pursed her lips.

"That doesn't make a bit of sense. She's the same Jen she has always been. Patsy, think about it and at least give her another chance. I've talked to her and I don't think there will be any problem in the future."

Sara went on. "Does this have anything to do with Greg?"

Patsy grumbled something unintelligible under her breath. She twisted the key in the lock on the small filing cabinet beneath her desk and pulled it out, dropping it in her pocket. Then she stood up, grabbed the sweater hanging on her chair and stalked out of the room.

That was funny, Jen thought. *Now what is SHE hiding?*

It wasn't long before Sara found out. Patsy's office adjoined Sara's, so it was easy just to call out her name and her Assistant would come running. The next morning she did this several times to no avail. She had talked to Patsy earlier so she knew she was around, but apparently she wasn't at her desk. Sara got up and took some paperwork out to lay it on Patsy's desk where she would find as soon as she returned. It was an urgent matter and needed to be taken care of right away.

As she laid the documents down, she perused Patsy's desk. What Sara saw shocked her. There were two plane tickets lying on top of a pile of papers. She picked them up to look at them. The top one was issued to Patricia Kline, scheduled departure in two days from Logan Airport to London Heathrow. The one underneath was issued to Gregory Smythe for the same flight.

Oh my God! They're running! Patsy must know all about it. Her heart sank. She would never have thought that of Patsy!

She slid Patsy's ticket back on top as it had been before and memorized the flight number. Then she took the papers she had brought out back into her office. Not in a million years did she want Patsy to know she had been out there and had seen the tickets. Her mind was spinning. What should she do? She wrote the flight number down on a pad of paper and hid it in her desk drawer.

She was nervous to do something about this situation immediately, but reason prevailed and she reached for her phone to call Maureen Sommerfield. She knew she should do nothing but alert the authorities. Otherwise, she might really boggle up their plans. Her mind was spinning in circles when Maureen's Assistant answered the phone. Unfortunately she said that Maureen was out.

"But it's really important," Sara urged. "Can't you patch me through to her? Can't you find her?"

The Assistant sighed. "I'm really sorry, Mrs. Jensen, but in all honesty, Ms. Sommerfield is at the dentist and it's the one thing that scares her to death so they knock her out. There's no way you can speak to her right now."

"Oh damn. Then please have her call me as soon as she can. Immediately, do you understand? It's extremely important!"

"I understand, Mrs. Jensen. I sure will."

Sara hung up the phone and put her head in her hands. It was so hard not to act! She wanted to lock them both in a closet and rip up the tickets! Her fear that they would get away was rising. Then she started talking to herself in her head. *Now just calm down. The tickets aren't for two more days. That's plenty of time to alert Maureen and for the SEC to act.* She felt let down and sick to her stomach to think that Patsy was involved in a scam.

When Maureen finally called back, her voice was soft and a little sluggish.

"Sorry that I missed your call, Sara. What can I do for you?"

Sara got up and closed her office door. Then she explained about finding the airline tickets and gave Maureen the flight number, destination and departure date.

Maureen's reaction was cold. "Well," she sighed. "That certainly doesn't make me very happy but I think we'll be OK. The sting was supposed to happen on Friday, but we can move it up to tomorrow if we scramble a bit. I would like to have a little more, but generally I think we've gathered enough information."

"Can you fill me in on the details?" Sara asked.

"NO", she said emphatically. The less you know the better. Just hang tight. Good-bye. I've gotta run and get busy on this."

"Good-bye," Sara said, resisting an urge to bite her nails.

Sara re-opened her door and heard Patsy rummaging around at her desk. She didn't feel like she could look at Patsy without suspicion so she waited until she had once again disappeared before she exited her office. Sara was leaving early. There was no way she could face her Assistant. She dropped the papers she had wanted to leave earlier and scribbled a quick note saying she had an appointment and had to leave early to place on top of them. Her exit was quick. As she walked out of their offices, she saw Patsy turning into Greg's office so she went the other way. There was no way she wanted to run in to her right now.

Sara's evening walk with Bogey was fast and he loved it. Her heart was racing with pent up energy. Hopefully this would all be over soon. The suspense was killing her.

Another restless night ensued. She didn't get to sleep until one a.m. Then Bogey let her know he had to go out at three am. She must remember to tell Katie not to give him so many treats! She got to sleep about 5 and overslept because she had forgotten to set her alarm. It was 9 before she groggily looked at the clock and then with a start, jumped out of bed.

CHAPTER TWENTY ONE

Greg was starting to get the feeling that something was going on. Over the past few days, he had the distinct impression he was being followed. He could never pinpoint anyone, but he found himself turning around to check when he was walking and constantly looking in his rear view mirror when he was driving.

Then there was that incident with Sara Jensen and the ledger book. How could he have walked off without it! Had she seen it? Did she know? Had she turned him in? He could swear that it was not **EXACTLY** where he had left it when he returned to get it. Damn! He was starting to get scared. This thing was big and he had the feeling it was about to implode.

That was why he purchased the airline tickets. He knew he had to take Patsy with him. He knew she loved him but that she would seek him out with a vengeance if he left her behind. She didn't know too much, but she was starting to get suspicious he was sure. She was asking too many questions.

Too bad that he didn't love her back. She was pretty enough and had a great figure, but she was a little too much of an airhead. It would be impossible to live with her. He would take care of her as soon as he got her out of the country. Good thing she was going so willingly! He laughed at his folly. It had been easy to convince her that it was a surprise romantic get-away and he knew she thought it would end with a surprise engagement ring. What an idiot!

That was when he started gathering his things. He made sure he had every shred of paper that could be used as evidence as well as the ledger book and trading receipts. He was combing his office for the last threads when there was a knock on the door. He heard Sara calling out his name. “Greg, may I come in?”

“Sure,” he called back, quickly shoving the things he had collected into a drawer. He looked up, but it wasn’t Sara who came in. The tall, attractive woman who entered introduced herself as Maureen Sommerfield, SEC agent. She was followed by two policemen wearing holsters and holding their hands out from their bodies as if they were ready to grab their guns. Sara followed.

Greg felt lucky that he was behind his desk. He put his hands in the air and said, “What’s all of this? I’m just going to sit down, OK? So we can talk.”

“Sure,” Maureen countered. “I think we have quite a lot to talk about.”

Greg sat down, lowered his hands and nodded, surprising Sara by clearly acknowledging that this was true.

Maureen went on. “Mr. Smythe. You are Greg Smythe. Correct?”

“Yes. Yes, of course.”

“Mr. Smythe, we are here to search your office.” Officer Harris had pulled a piece of paper out of his pocket and was handing it to Greg. “That piece of paper is a warrant that gives us full authority.”

Greg was turning white and simply nodded. “OK,” he choked out. “Where would you like to start?”

“With your desk,” Maureen replied. “How about if you slowly start opening your desk drawers and putting everything you find there on top?”

Greg nodded and steeled himself. He took a small ring of keys out of his breast pocket and leaned over to open the bottom left drawer first. Standing on the other side of the desk, the group couldn’t see the contents.

Without hesitating, he grabbed the loaded gun he kept there and pointed it at his chest. Before anyone could move, he pulled the trigger. There was a sharp crack and Sara and Maureen both involuntarily screamed. The amount of blood spurting from the wound was horrifying. It seemed like it was everywhere.

Greg fell off his chair and hit the floor. The two policemen rushed to his side and Officer Harris applied pressure to the wound with his hands. Officer Davis pulled out his police radio and called for an ambulance.

Patsy heard the shot and came running. When she saw Greg, she screamed and burst into tears. She ran to him, and got on her knees to cradle his head, trying to stay out of the way of the officers who were stabilizing the wound. Miraculously, he was still alive.

Greg whispered to Patsy, “It’s entirely my fault. I’ll try and get you out of this.”

“What? What are you talking about?” she cried. “I have no idea what you are talking about!”

Greg lapsed into unconsciousness. Patsy cried harder and held his hand the whole time they loaded him onto a stretcher. When they carried him out, she followed in her blood stained dress.

CHAPTER TWENTY TWO

Maureen had forgotten to inform him about her change in plans, so Jake had been out of the office at the time of the shooting.

Sara was sitting in his office waiting for him when he returned and she recounted the whole event before he even had time to take off his coat. When he heard what had happened, he was visibly upset – livid that Maureen had come with a warrant when he was away – livid that he had not been informed – and also extremely concerned for Greg's safety and Patsy's well-being. He was always such a pillar of strength. It unnerved Sara to see him so rattled.

"So long story short," she finished. "Greg is on life support at Boston Memorial. Patsy is there with him. "What shall we do?"

"I don't know," he said. "I have no fucking idea." He rubbed his eyes. "I never pegged Greg for this. How could he do this? And how could Patsy be interested in somebody like that?"

"Maybe it's easier for me to understand," Sara said. "It has been a long time since anyone has shown any interest in Patsy. She's getting older. He's very handsome and articulate. She thought he was successful. She probably thought she was in love and loved back and she didn't see his shallow side. It's like they say. Love is blind."

"I feel helpless, Jake. I should have seen this coming. In retrospect, there were a lot of clues."

"I do too, Sara."

He walked over, leaned down and gave her a hug. "It's not your fault, Sara. I'm sorry. I was just so shocked."

"Come on. Let's go to the hospital," he said. "Get your coat and we'll ride together."

CHAPTER TWENTY THREE

Both Jake and Sara were silent during the trip to Boston Memorial. When they arrived, they found out at the front desk that Greg was in the Operating Room. Lucky for him, the bullet had missed his heart, but it had shattered a rib and lodged in the heart cavity wall so it needed to be removed. Things were going well with the operation and he was expected to be moved to the Critical Care section in a few hours.

They went to the cafeteria and picked at some lunch, then up to the Critical Care Nurse's Station where they were greeted by a cute redhead named Kristi. She was wearing a red and white striped apron and couldn't be perkier. She listened to their explanations of who they were and pulled out Greg's chart. She directed them to the Waiting Room where they found a teary eyed Patsy blowing her nose, sitting off in a corner beside a large pile of used Kleenex.

Sara felt conflicted seeing Patsy like that. On one hand she was angry that Patsy had gotten involved with Greg and that she hadn't known anything about it. She was angry thinking that Patsy could possibly have known what Greg was doing. It seemed plausible since she had a plane ticket to leave with him. But on the other hand she felt sorry for her. Patsy was a longtime friend and devoted employee. It was really hard to believe she wasn't completely innocent and simply a woman in love. At any rate, it didn't seem an appropriate time to ask.

The look on Sara's face was completely sympathetic as she approached Patsy. She sat down beside her and put her arm around her. Jake sat next to her, mute, letting Sara handle the situation. That triggered a new round of sobbing. Sara dropped her arm and she and Jake sat quietly while Patsy calmed down.

Sara found herself praying that Greg would survive. She prayed Greg's name but underneath it all, she knew she was praying for herself. She felt selfish, but if Greg died she might never find out about Peter's account that was right in the middle of Greg's scam. She might never be able to reconcile her reeling thoughts and doubts about her husband – the man she had thought she could trust. It was as if another rug had been pulled out from under her feet.

Sara just wanted to go home, to snuggle with Bogey, then to crawl in bed and sleep a deep and comforting sleep, waking up to find out that it was all a dream.

Just then, the ER Operating Physician entered. He had a sad look on his face, reporting that the overall operation had gone well, but that there was so much damage that the overall outlook was grim. "We'll just have to wait and see," he said. "It's all in God's hands now. There is nothing more I can do but keep him comfortable."

"Can we see him soon?" Patsy asked.

The doctor sighed. "Yes, but I want you to be prepared that his psyche is not good. He's just waking up in the Recovery Room and all he said was to please let him die."

"I just don't understand," Patsy said, dissolving into a new puddle of tears.

The doctor put his hand on her shoulder. "I'm sorry ma'am. Let me know if there is anything I can do for you. And if there's anything we can do for him, you know we will. I just don't know what it is at the moment. If you can help him to regain his will to live, that could mean a lot. Good luck."

"Oh God," Sara thought. "Now Patsy is going to blame herself for that. Damn."

Sara knew that investigators would be coming soon, so they had no choice but to fill Patsy in on their discoveries. She kept balling up her fists as she listened, nothing short of incredulous.

When she was finished, Sara was convinced that Patsy had known nothing about the scam. “He was – is – no good, Patsy.” You have to break free.

“Sara, Jake – Is this really true?” She looked from one to the other.

Jake nodded and Sara said, “I’m afraid so, Patsy. We’re going to go now. Are you all right?”

Then it was Patsy’s turn to nod. They left her there, staring at a wall.

CHAPTER TWENTY FOUR

A group of SEC investigators led by Maureen Sommerfield wasted no time going through Greg's apartment and then his office. The office especially was a boon. It didn't take them long to find the stash of documents he had been about to take off with. They silently thanked him for making their jobs easier by gathering it all together.

Maureen stopped by Sara's office to tell her the news.

"We have enough on him to put him away for a long time."

"I could guess that just from what I saw in the ledger. Can you believe the names in there? CEO's from the biggest firms in the country."

"I know. They have to already be making some pretty big salaries. The fact that they were colluding and insider trading is simply greedy."

Sara shook her head and sighed. "It never ends, does it? You can never imagine what otherwise good people will do for money."

"You're right, but a lot of it has to do with your occupation. It's just so easy."

Sara nodded again. “It’s a big temptation I guess. But luckily one I’ve never had.”

“Keep it that way!” Maureen admonished, raising her eyebrows with a quick nod.

“Don’t worry!” Sara grinned. “Keep in touch, OK?”

“I will. Hopefully we’ll be able to depose Greg soon.”

Greg was intubated and drugged into a coma to promote healing so he was unreachable for a long time. Sara called the Nursing Station daily to stay informed – to be sure she would talk to him at the very first opportunity.

It was almost four weeks before he could be deposed. By then, he was able to sit up and was clear headed enough to realize how much trouble he was in.

Maureen did indeed keep them informed and Sara and Jake were in the waiting room while it was going on. She knèw they were there and came by when it was over.

“So how did it go?” Jake asked. “I’m looking forward to telling him he’s fired if he hasn’t figured it out already.”

Maureen almost laughed. “Try not to be too bitter,” Maureen replied. “I’m sure he knows that and it’s a very minor part of his problems. He's in a hell of a lot of trouble and pinned to the wall. No jury is going to let him off the hook. He did try to strike a bargain for information though. Which is funny because we have it all already due to his meticulous records. They have come back totally to bite him."

"Is he remorseful at all?" Sara asked.

"Well, I don't know. He seemed to be, but I think he's a very good actor. How else could he have gotten this caliber of people to participate in his scheme?"

"Do you think they all really knew what they were getting into?"

"Yes, Sara. How could they not? They are all high level, intelligent people. Perhaps they could have fooled themselves into ignoring it, but they will all be brought in and they'll have a hell of a time convincing a jury that they were innocently taken advantage of. You just don't get those kinds of quick profits legally. It's insane what they did."

"You can go in and see him now if you like. It's probably a good time. He'll be glad to get it all over with. Go fire him, Jake. He deserves it and I know you will enjoy it."

"Yes, I think I will enjoy it. Come on, Sara. Let's go talk to the creep."

When they got in the room, Greg was half sitting up in bed, leaning against three pillows and staring at the wall. When their eyes met, both of the men's feelings were written all over their faces. Jake was plenty mad at what Greg had done to his firm and its reputation. Greg was frightened but stubborn and trying not to show it, which made him appear cocky and made Jake even madder. Knowing how angry he was and how defenseless Greg was, Jake decided to let Sara speak first so he would have a chance to calm down.

Sara took a deep breath. Her imagination was running wild about Peter.

"So Greg. Hey. How are you doing?"

"How do you **THINK** I'm doing, Sara? What are you two doing here anyway?"

"I want information. Information that I think I deserve," she said determinedly.

"And what would that be pray tell?" he said sarcastically. "I think the SEC has everything you need."

"No, not that, Greg. It's Peter. I want to know what Peter's involvement was in this."

"Oh, of course. Peter. Why don't you ask him?"

"Peter's dead, Greg. Or did you forget that?" she said testily.

"No, of course not. I just wanted to hurt you."

"Thank you," she said sarcastically. "I can't imagine why…"

He interrupted. "If it wasn't for you, none of this would have happened."

"Pardon me?"

"You meddled in my business and the whole thing came crashing down. Until then, a lot of people were happy making money and nobody was getting hurt. It was helping the stock market out, the firm out, me out and nobody was getting hurt by it. Now a lot of people are going to get hurt. You're a jealous idiot."

With that, Jake started to move toward Greg, clenching his fist.

Sara grabbed his arm. "Jake! Stop! He'll get his and believe me I'm not offended. It's pretty easy to consider the source," she said angrily.

"Let's get ourselves under control here. Come on, Greg. I need to know about Peter's involvement."

"Money," Greg sneered. "Money was all any of us wanted. He made a lot and I take it you didn't know about it."

"No, I didn't know about it. That's perfectly correct. But I want to know where the money came from that he did this with. And how do you two know each other anyway?"

"College. We met playing poker with a bunch of guys. I've known him a long time. When I started this investment deal, I looked him up. At first I didn't know he was your husband, but when I found out and he found out I was with Jordon, we decided to keep it quiet."

"I didn't know any of that," she said, redundantly, more for herself than anyone else.

"Well, maybe you don't know a lot of things."

"I guess I don't," she said morosely. "Then just tell me where the money came from, why it was put in an account somewhere else and why I knew nothing about it."

"I have no clue where the money he invested with me came from," he replied. "I guess you'll never know if you can't ask Peter. Evidently your relationship wasn't as great as you thought," he sneered. "I just know he gave it to me to invest because I was damn good at it. I wired his profits into that account because he was my client and he asked me to. That's all. I guess it's obvious that he didn't want you to know about it but that's all I can tell you. It wasn't any of my business. My only job was to make money for him."

She shook her head. "Greed. It's all about greed. You were a bunch of greedy Bastards. "

"Bravo, Sara. I've never heard you swear. But hey, I resent that," Greg replied. I made money for those people and they liked it. Everyone is responsible for their own greed. That's why it was so easy for me. Because they were greedy. I just did what they wanted and then they wanted more and more and more - and so it goes. Now you know the rest of the story – well most of it." He looked at Sara. "I guess **YOU** don't know everything you want to know, but I can't help you with that."

"So you had no greed of your own?" Jake interjected.

Greg didn't answer. He rolled his eyes and gave them a dismissive look. He was silent for a minute and then said, "And I suppose you don't, Mr. Puritan. You seemed to like my production pretty well."

"I can't deny that, but I had no idea that it wasn't on the up and up. You know I can't let you get away with this."

Greg frowned and pinched his eyes together. "It's a little too late to say that, I think. I believe everything is already out in the open. As you know, I won't be the only one going down."

Sara was heartbroken. She thought she would get her answers. Today. Now. Wondering was eating her alive. She gave up and sat down in a visitor's chair next to the wall, looking completely defeated.

Jake took the cue and picked up where she left off. "Look, Greg. I can't believe you jeopardized my firm with your scheme. Not to mention our reputation. I had faith in you and you took advantage of my trust."

"Hey, what's going on here? You two blast in here and take advantage of a sick man who can't defend himself? Who let you in here anyway?" He hit his CALL button and a nurse quickly appeared.

"Please get these two out of here," he said grabbing his chest. "They're upsetting me."

"All right. Out of here," she said.

Greg sneered again. "And don't let them in here again. Start making a list," he ordered. "I don't want anybody in here who doesn't have to be."

"Sure," the nurse said soothingly. "No problem."

As Sara and Jake walked out of the room, Jake threw back in a testy voice, “Oh, and PS. You’re fired.”

Sara couldn’t help but smirk. Outside, she was the first to speak. “Well, that sure went well,” she said sarcastically.

“Yeah. But what do you expect? At the moment, I’m not sure why we came.”

“Because we wanted answers! Because I wanted answers! I still want answers” she cried out.

“Well, there aren’t any,” Jake replied. “We’re just going to have to live with that. Let’s go back to the office, straighten up his mess and then forget about him.”

At that point, all Sara was thinking about was what she would say to Jen.

CHAPTER TWENTY FIVE

Sara waited until the next morning to call her niece. She set her alarm and got up early because she knew she couldn't let Jen hear what had happened from anyone else.

Jen groggily answered the phone, but perked up as soon as she heard it was her aunt and what the topic was. Sara went through it all and Jen asked a few questions, but not as many as Sara had feared. She deliberately left out Peter's involvement because she wasn't yet sure how he fit in and she literally didn't know what to say.

"Well, I guess that's it then," Jen finally said.

Sara paused. "You sound miffed?"

"No, not miffed, just glad it's all over." Jen yawned.

"OK, well… I just wanted to hear it from me."

"Yeah. Thanks. I appreciate it. Really, Aunt Sara. It's no big deal to me. I just wanted him to be caught. Disappointed I didn't catch him, but I'm glad you did."

Sara could hear her smiling and believed her. "OK then. See you at the office!"

"See you at the office. Onward and upward."

Sara could hear her smiling and knew that all was well. Her niece was still hanging on the phone though, so she said, “Don’t play Nancy Drew again, OK?”

“OK. Lesson learned,” said Jen and they both hung up their phones.

The office buzzed about the events for weeks, but eventually things settled down and business resumed as normal.

Sara was just about to ring Patsy when she walked in. “Speak of the devil,” she said. “I was just going to ask you to come in to do some letters with me. I know I usually do them myself but I don’t have time. Can I just tell you the gist of what I want to say and can you whip them together for me? I need to leave soon to see a client and I want to get them out later today.”

Patsy looked morose, as was usual lately, but she tried to smile and said “Sure. You know I need to keep busy. I’m just having a terrible time getting over Greg.”

“Tell me about it.”

“Oh Sara. I’m so sorry. That was thoughtless of me.”

"Just be glad you're not going to jail with him, Patsy. It could have been even worse."

"I know, but it's still hard. I loved him."

"Well you know what they say. Love is blind." Sara's voice was hardening. There was that saying again. She knew that she also had to apply that to herself. She also knew it wasn't fair to take it out on Patsy. Even though it was hard to believe, she was perfectly innocent in any of Greg's crimes.

Sara sighed. To her surprise, Patsy continued to apologize.

"Look, Sara. I'm so sorry about the things I said about Jen. I mean… I just couldn't see straight when it came to Greg. Jealousy really is an ugly thing. I knew he was attracted to Jen and I couldn't handle it. I convinced myself that she was after him and blamed her for everything. The petty cash thing could have been anyone. It was wrong of me to accuse her and I really regret it."

"I'm glad you see that now, Patsy. Maybe you could find a way to apologize to her?"

Patsy nodded.

Sara went on. "I suppose you were drawn to his good looks. He really is quite handsome."

"Maybe initially, but it was much more than that. He's quite a nice person. He was so kind to me and treated me like a lady all the time. He didn't seem to have any agenda except to make me happy and to love me." She threw up her hands. "In my mind, he was simply a dream come true."

"Do you feel like you still love him? Even now?"

"No. Not at all. I could never love a criminal. I'm just still reeling from the surprise and from the hurt. I can't believe I let myself be duped like that. I mean, I thought I **KNEW** him like the back of my hand. When I think of how I trusted him I want to puke. I was such a fool."

"I'm sorry too, Patsy. I should have trusted you more. I should have talked to you more. I'm sorry you had to go through all of this by yourself and I can well imagine how shattering it is now. You were taken advantage of in a big way – the worst way."

"That's nice of you to say, but I'm sure it wouldn't have made any difference. I just hope we can get through this without it hurting our relationship."

"I think we can," Sara said softly. In fact, why don't we forget all of this right now? Why don't you take a vacation? I think you could use some time off and when you come back we can start all over again. We'll finish up most of these files this week, so why don't you go next Monday? You've got unused vacation time and Jen can help me while you're gone. I would enjoy spending more time with her anyway and it will give me a chance to talk more with her on where we go from here. Isn't there some place you've been dying to visit?"

"Actually, yes. And I think that's a good idea. I've wanted to go to the Bahamas for a long time. It's funny because I get Expedia alerts and I just noticed there are some specials on flights there. I'm glad you mentioned it because I've been thinking about going away too and I'm absolutely ready to do it. If you really don't mind, I will. Thank you. I'll just do it all by myself. I'll go book the flight as soon as we get through these letters you want me to write.

"Deal," said Sara. "You need it. Go." She was happy to see that Patsy's spirits seemed lifted. *At least someone's were,* she thought.

CHAPTER TWENTY SIX

Patsy ended up leaving two weeks later. When she landed in the Bahamas, the weather was balmy and beautiful. Suddenly, she didn't even mind being alone. Perhaps she would meet someone. *Maybe I should hang out at the bar*, she thought recklessly.

The villa she had rented was lovely with its pristine, white walls and colorful flowers. From her living room window, she looked out at a sandy beach and turquoise blue water. *Paradise!* She thought. After unpacking, she quickly rubbed on sun block and then changed into a bright, flowered sundress. She picked up her sunglasses and a straw hat and headed for the beach. She found a comfortable lounge chair and sat there for hours, sipping glasses of Chardonnay brought to her by a waiter from the beach bar and languishing in the warm sunshine. There was nothing more peaceful than reading and in the background, listening to the waves quietly lapping against the shore.

That chair soon became her favorite spot. Each day, through the main hotel, she signed up for a different excursion. She did some shopping and made a few friends to share dinner with. But each afternoon, she returned to her lounge chair on the beach to unwind. This afternoon was no different, until she saw him.

It was getting close to dinner time. He was thinner than she remembered and he had grown a beard. The beard was nicely trimmed and he was dressed in light tan slacks and a black and tan Tommy Bahama floral shirt. He wore brown loafers with no socks. Patsy held her breath as he walked by, smiling and chatting with an attractive woman. He put his hand on the woman's back as he guided her up toward the bar. The gesture was obviously very familiar.

No. Impossible. It couldn't be. I'm imagining things, she thought. *I've had too much to drink!* Patsy kept her head down and tipped her hat to hide her face as they passed. She followed them out of the corner of her eye and once they had reached the bar, she stood up and looked directly at them from a different angle. *Yes, there's no doubt. It's him.* ***PETER****. Peter is alive and Peter is here, right in front of my eyes.*

Patsy was too unnerved to go to the bar herself. Thoughts were racing through her mind. *I should confront him! What will Sara do? How can this be possible? Peter is* ***DEAD!*** *How can I possibly tell Sara? Would it be better if I just forgot about this? I'm crazy. This can't be true. It must be someone who simply looks a lot like Peter – a doppelganger.*

I should just talk to him and get over this improbable machination.

Unable to reconcile her thoughts, she went to her room and ordered room service. When it arrived, it looked good, but she couldn't touch a bite. She watched the news and then tried to watch one of her favorite television programs, but ended up doing more pacing than watching. Finally she left the food, outside her door untouched.

During the four vacation days Patsy had left, she tried to distract herself by keeping busy. Reading was out of the question. She couldn't concentrate. Instead, she booked all the excursions she could find. She went snorkeling. She visited a turtle farm. She even tried turtle soup, which wasn't so bad once she got past the idea of it. She went wind surfing, doing everything with groups of tourists who were outgoing and friendly distractions.

She avoided sitting at the bar, but saw him three more times before she left. It was always at dinnertime. Sometimes he was alone and sometimes he was met by the same woman. *Maybe he's on vacation too?* But somehow that didn't seem right. From his tan, his clothing and his demeanor, it was more realistic to think that he lived nearby. It just didn't feel like he was on vacation. Everyone at the bar seemed to know him well. He didn't spend time on the beach, didn't show up in any excursion lines and only appeared to have drinks or eat at the hotel. By the time she left for home, she was convinced. The only thing to figure out now was how to tell Sara.

Sara had more problems of her own. While Patsy was gone, the partial print came back with a hit. Sara got a call from Officer Maxman with the news. The culprit was one Alberto Abondonato, a local Italian. They had not been able to find him to question him, but he was a known mobster with a record. He made sure that he asked Sara if everything had been OK since the break-in.

*No, everything is **NOT OK**,* she thought. But in direct answer to his question she could only reply yes. He said they would keep looking and would be in touch.

CHAPTER TWENTY SEVEN

Jake knocked on the casing of Sara's open office door and stuck his head in. She looked up at his grin and completely melted. *Why hadn't she noticed how handsome he was? Really handsome. Really kind. Really everything.* Over the past year and a half since Peter's death, they had spent a lot of time together. They had been friends for a long time and he had always been there as one of her supporters. It was all completely natural and completely innocent. But suddenly it seemed different. He had gone from friend to something much more special.

"Sara, I've come to distract you," he said teasingly. "You need to get out of here. Let's go and get some dinner. It's seven o'clock. You have to be hungry! You're nothing but skin and bones. I bet you haven't had a decent meal in weeks except when we've gone to lunch. No, it must be months. Whaddaya say? I took the liberty of making a reservation at Meritage. Thought you might enjoy looking out over the water. I've got a table by the window."

"I say, OK, you're right and I'm hungry. Perfect timing." She stood up, grabbed her purse and sweater and said, "Let's go. Let's go now before I change my mind." He smiled and as they exited the building, he took her arm. His touch caused electricity to run through her body. She didn't remember that happening before. *What was suddenly so different? She was falling for him. That was it. She was in love with him. Simply that and it made her feel guilty, even though Peter had been gone for so long.*

The restaurant was packed. The noise level was a bit high but neither of them cared. Sara was noticing things she hadn't really noticed before. He was completely intent on her – totally interested in every single thing she had to say. She told him about the call about the fingerprint from the police and how she had been feeling about all that had happened. She found herself relaxing and enjoying herself immensely. Jake ordered a bottle of Melville Chardonnay and they sipped it as they looked through the menu, choosing pan seared diver scallops with pea greens and pink grapefruit butter first, to share. After that, it was wood grilled Filet Mignon with soft whipped potatoes and horseradish onion cream Meritage syrup for him and steamed lobster tail with snap peas and Satsuma Tangerine Essence for her. The service was excellent, their conversation was animated and they finished up the Chardonnay as they finished the appetizer.

Jake asked for the wine menu again and ordered a glass of Catena Zapata Malbec from Argentina for each of them, knowing it was one of her favorites. The food was exquisite and despite being full, they ordered chocolate pumpkin mouse cake to share for dessert. He ordered two glasses of Raymond-Lafon Sauternes to pair with it. The sweet wine slid down her throat like candied syrup. *This evening is magical,* she thought. *Or maybe it's just the wine? No, it's magical.* She looked into his eyes and saw not only a best friend, but someone she would like to continue to spend a lot of time with.

Lingering over the Sauternes, their eyes met in a different way than ever before. She thought she could see a lot of caring in those eyes and she liked it. When they finally left the restaurant, Jake drove her home. When he pulled up in front of her house, no one moved. They had been sitting in the car talking for fifteen minutes when she asked him if he would like to come in for a nightcap. In answer, he put his arm around her and pulled her close, kissing her for the first time. When she finally broke away, he opened his car door and came around to open hers. He followed her into the house. As soon as the front door closed, they melted into each other's arms.

CHAPTER TWENTY EIGHT

When Sara woke up the next morning, Jake was propped up on one elbow looking at her. "Hey!" she said. "That's not fair!"

"What's not fair?"

"You can't look at me when I'm not looking at you!"

"What? Why not?" he asked, with a fake look of shock on his face.

"I don't have any make-up on. I've been sleeping. I must look…" He smothered her next words with a kiss. Then he said, "Oh Sara. You are so beautiful. I have been blind."

She kissed him again. "I feel the same way, Jake. We were just in different parts of our lives. It didn't make sense then, but it does now. I'm ready to accept 'things' and move on. I'm sure I am."

He just smiled and rolled over on top of her. They made love again. It was swift and wonderful and she didn't want it to end. Afterward, they lay spoon style without speaking for close to half an hour. His arms felt so warm, strong and loving around her. She was almost falling asleep again when he said, "Sara, I love you. I can't help it. I think I always have."

Her response was immediate. “I love you too, Jake. You have been my best friend for a long time – in many different kinds of ways.” She turned around to hold him again and the kiss was passionate.

“Jake, there’s something I’ve been thinking about.”

“What’s that, darling?”

“Do you like kids?”

“Sure. I like kids.”

“Why didn’t you ever have any?”

“I wasn’t able to. I’m sterile. I’ve always wanted them though. I feel like there’s an unfulfilled hole in my life. Not that I dwell on it, but there has always been something missing.”

“Oh. That would explain it.”

“I think I know why you’re asking though.”

“And why is that?”

“I can tell you in one word and it’s Marta.”

Her face lit up as she smiled at him and wonderfully, so did his. “Yes. You’re absolutely right. I’ve fallen in love with her too.” She paused and looked him in the eye. “But how did you know?”

"Your spy, Patsy, has been keeping me informed He laughed. "If I look at the amount of time you have been spending with her, it's pretty clear. She seems like a wonderful little girl. I've seen the pictures on your desk. I can totally understand and I think I've fallen in love with her vicariously through you." He smiled a sweet, understanding smile that melted her heart. He went on. "Do you want to adopt her?"

"Yes," she said without hesitation. Then more carefully, lowering her head but looking up at him. "Would you support me on that?"

He hugged her again. "Of course. In more ways than you know."

She looked up at him gratefully and an unspoken commitment hung between them. They kissed again, a long and lingering kiss that bonded their hearts together.

Sara reluctantly pulled away to look at the clock, then smiled and said softly, "We had better get to work."

"I know," he said. "I hate to, but I know you're right."

They showered together, then got dressed and went into the office separately – and late. Sara felt incredibly happy. She felt so close to Jake that it was almost as if he was sitting beside her as she drove. She decided that the best thing she liked about him was his laugh. He had an honest, belly laugh that shook his sides. While he was laughing, he looked you right in the eye so you couldn't tear your eyes away and you simply had to laugh with him. You could tell a lot about a person by the way they laughed.

She was smiling as she entered the office because she was also looking forward to seeing Patsy on her first day back from vacation. Sara had missed her. Things never ran quite as smoothly when Patsy was gone. Plus she was a friend. Someone Sara could always rely on. There was a lot to be said for that.

Patsy took one look at her and said, "Wow. What happened while I was gone? You look like a new woman!" Sara laughed. "Nothing, really. Just trying to be happy for a change. How about you? Did you have a good vacation?"

"Yes, it was wonderful. Hard to believe I could have such a good time all by myself. I joined in with a lot of groups and it was good for me to relax and have some fun." The tone of her voice belied her words, but Sara didn't even notice as she said, "We've got a lot of catching up to do. Let's get busy!" as she walked into her office.

The day was busy and Sara was in and out. Before they both knew it, it was almost time for Patsy to leave. "Sara, are you about ready to leave the office?"

"Sure, Patsy. Why?"

"Well, I was wondering if we could stop and have a drink after work."

"Sure! That would be fun. You can tell me all about your vacation."

"Yes, that's what I want to do" Patsy said carefully. "That's exactly what I want to do."

Sara looked at her quizzically. Something seemed odd about her attitude. *Was she worried about something? All the more reason to go relax and have a drink. Then it will all come out.*

They headed over to The Forum and sat at the bar. Patsy started telling Sara all about her vacation but she didn't seem happy. Sara finally said, "Patsy, what's wrong? I know you too well to think anything otherwise. Tell me. How can I help?"

To Sara's surprise, Patsy started crying.

It took a good ten minutes for Patsy to get herself under control. Then she looked up at Sara pitifully and simply said, "Peter is alive."

"What?" Sara almost yelled. "That's not the least bit funny. What's wrong with you? How could you do this to me?"

"I'm sorry, Sara, but it's true. You know I would never do anything to hurt you. I saw him for myself. I saw him multiple times. I know it was him. He is living in the Bahamas near Nassau."

"Oh for God's sake, Patsy. Your imagination is running absolutely wild. I can't believe this!"

"At first I didn't either, but Sara, it's true. I know it's true. Trust me, I didn't want to believe it, but I saw him with my own eyes. He was with a woman. He's alive, Sara. He's alive."

Sara fished in her purse and pulled out enough money to pay the drink bill and a tip. She threw it on the counter, stood up and said, "I don't believe you. Stay away from me. This is a cruel prank." Her head was reeling as she stomped out the bar and drove home.

She let her lovable Bogey outside and then measured chopped meat, cottage cheese and string beans into his dog dish. When he came back in, she fed him and then sat on the floor and hugged him for a long time.

Underneath it all, she had doubts. She had doubts because she did not believe Patsy could lie to her.

She could not believe Patsy was capable of making this up. She could only wonder. *Could it be possible? They never did find a body. Could it really be possible? Oh my God. What a difference a day makes. What shall I do?*

CHAPTER TWENTY NINE

Sara told Jake she reluctantly had too much to do to get together again that evening. She needed time to think but was still in a tailspin when she arrived at the office the next day. He stopped by several times, but she feigned being too busy to talk. Her head was swimming. She wasn't ready. *What could she possibly say? I love you but oh, my husband is alive and I'll see you later?* She did love him. That was the problem. That was the whole problem.

At the end of the day, Jake stopped back. He said he wanted to come home with her and this time she said OK. There was no way this could be discussed in the office. They needed to be somewhere private.

Sara left first. When she arrived, she let Bogey out and fed him, then looked in the wine fridge for a bottle. It was empty, so she took a deep breath and headed downstairs to the wine cellar. She hated to enter because it had been Peter's hobby more than her own and it felt like the cellar was his precious sanctuary. There was no other place in the house where memories of him were stronger. She hadn't been able to shake the feeling that he was omnipresent there.

What to drink? Something that can stand alone, she thought. That usually meant Zinfandel – always the fruity palate pleaser. Never crying out for food to make it happier like some others that needed that support. Since she didn't have any food to offer, it seemed like a perfect choice. She grabbed a box and filled it with six bottles of different Zins to refill the wine fridge and hurried up the stairs. She chose a bottle of Carlisle and put the other five in the fridge, tossing the box aside. When the Carlisle was uncorked she smelled it lovingly, then pulled two glasses out of the cupboard and filled one. Leaning against the kitchen counter, she downed it for courage and poured another.

Lost in thought, Sara suddenly realized that Jake was at the back door, ringing the bell and looking at her through the glass. She put her glass down and opened the door to a big bear hug that took her feet off the floor. The hug unnerved her and she lost all of her inhibitions. The tears started to flow.

"Hey, hey. Hush. What's wrong here sweetheart?" He sat her down on a kitchen bar stool and placed her glass of wine in front of her. While she calmed down, he poured one for himself, sat down on a stool beside her and took a few sips. "Mmmmm. Love a woman that can choose a good glass of wine." He smiled, tentatively. "So what's wrong? Spill."

"I don't know where to begin," she said.

"Then just tell me. It can't be all that bad. Did you lose Jimmy Frank's office pool?"

"That's not funny," she replied tearfully.

"Sorry. Really. Sorry. What is it?"

Then she simply blurted it out. "Peter's alive!"

"What in the hell? That's not funny, Sara. What are you talking about?" He looked crestfallen.

While she was relating Patsy's story, he poured himself a glass of wine and stood sipping it. When she finished, he was completely silent for a few minutes. Then he set his glass down and finally said, "You really believe this, don't you?"

"I'm not sure. I want to but I don't want to. I don't know what I want. I can't wish ill on him, but I thought he was dead! I love you, but he's my husband," she said. "I don't know what to do. The timing for all of this is hysterical, isn't it? Even 48 hours ago I might have felt totally different. But now you're in my life in a big way and I'm so confused."

She paused, gathering her courage again. "I feel like I have to go and see for myself. I have to go down there and try to find him."

"OK" he said decisively. "I'll go with you. I'll look into tickets. Pack your bags," he said and walked out the door.

Sara's emotions were running rampant. Part of her wanted Jake to go with her. Part of her didn't. Part of her believed Peter was alive. Part of her didn't. Part of her wanted Peter to be alive. Part of her didn't. The whole thing was an impossible situation.

One thing she did know, though, was that she had to tell Jen. Her hand was shaking as she dialed her niece's number. Luckily Jen was home and picked up on the second ring.

"Hi Aunt Sara!" she said. "What's up?"

Sara held the phone tightly.

"Look Jen. There's something I would rather tell you in person, but I don't want to make you drive over here and I've had some wine so I don't want to drive over there."

"Gee, Aunt Sara. Are you OK? This sounds serious."

"It is serious, Jen, and I don't know how to couch this so I'm just going to blurt it out. We think Uncle Peter is alive," she said helplessly.

"Really? No joke? That's impossible! How? What are you talking about?" Jen was incredulous.

"I'm not surprised at your reaction. Mine was the same."

"But that's wonderful! But how could it be? Do you mean he wasn't in the building when it was bombed?"

"I don't know, Jen. I wish I could give you those answers. I wish I had them myself. Believe me. I would like for the whole puzzle to be solved right this minute because it's so crazy to try and think about it. But unfortunately I don't have any details. I promise to let you know as soon as I know anything, OK?"

"OK. Sure. But how did you find this out and when will he be home?"

"You know that Patsy was just on vacation in the Bahamas and she thinks she saw him. I suppose it's possible that it wasn't him, but Patsy knows him pretty well and she certainly wouldn't tell me this if she didn't absolutely believe it."

"You mean Patsy just ran into him? He didn't come to you? You mean he took off? Have you talked to him? When is he coming home? Jen was talking in circles, trying to imagine what could have happened.

"Jen, please try to understand. I have to see for myself if it's him and then if it is I have to talk to him myself. It has been a long time and I have no idea what could be going on in his head. After all this time, maybe he doesn't want to come home. I have to consider that."

"That couldn't possibly be true!" she cried. "You can't do this alone. I'll go with you!"

"No Jen. Again, please try to understand. This is something I have to do alone. I don't even know how I feel about it and I love you dearly but it would complicate things to have you along. Like I said, I promise to call you as soon as I know anything. In the meantime, try not to get too excited just in case it isn't true or in case of lots of things, OK?" Sara decided on the spot not to tell her about Jake or that Jake was going with her. It was too much at once.

"OK. I understand. I think I do anyway. It's pretty big stuff though. You have to admit."

"I know, Jen. Just try and hold this thought until I can give you more information."

"OK. I gotta go now. I gotta call my mom!"

Oh great, Sara thought. *But of course she would need to call her mom.* So she just said "OK" and "We'll talk soon" and hung up the phone.

Corinne was on her mind now. *What would her sister say?* She wouldn't answer her phone that night. She didn't want to talk to Corinne right now. She knew Corinne loved her and this would hit her hard, but she had nothing to say and didn't want to listen to any lectures. There would be plenty of time to talk about it later. Corinne would just have to wait.

She struggled with that thought though. She wasn't sure that would be fair to Corinne and was questioning her decision when her phone rang and Jake's name popped up.

"We're all set," he said determinedly. "I've booked two tickets to Nassau for tomorrow morning. We'll have to leave about 4:30 am to get to the airport in time because the flight leaves at 6:20. Sorry that it's so early, but there's no good way to get there quickly.

"Already?" she said. "I'm still getting used to this idea. And getting tickets on such short notice must have cost a fortune!"

"I don't care. I don't give a hoot about the money. We may as well get it over with. Not knowing is already driving me crazy and I'm sure it is you too. Let's just go and do the thing," he said firmly.

"I'm in my car now on the way to your place. It will be easier than adding more time having to pick you up in the morning."

"OK," she answered weakly. "I guess you're right. There's no denying that we have to get to the bottom of this and it does make sense for you to stay here. I just feel so guilty about it."

"Don't," he said with conviction. "See you soon, honey."

"See you soon." Her voice was shaky because she didn't know what to do. Thank God he was being strong. Thank God somebody was.

As she hit the call end button on her phone, she was filled with a sense of dread. What were they in for? Only time would tell.

CHAPTER THIRTY

Jake held Sara's hand tightly as the plane pulled away from the loading dock. They were on an American flight, leaving at 6:20 am that would get into Nassau at 1:29 pm. It had been difficult to find a flight without a terribly long layover, especially on such short notice, but Jake had managed something reasonable. Under any circumstances, it was a long trip. They settled in for the ride. Both felt like they should be talking things through, but neither spoke. What was there to say? The end of this story hinged on whether Patsy was right, and if she was, neither knew for sure how they would react.

The pilot landed the plane effortlessly in Nassau in beautiful weather. As they deplaned into the bright sunshine, Sara looked up at her handsome traveling partner and tried to smile. Her mind circled around one thought. *If only the circumstances were different!* Somehow she had to get herself out of this mess with her dignity intact.

Their villa was booked in the same complex where Patsy had stayed. It was as beautiful as Patsy had described. Sara had initially said they should get separate rooms just in case, but Jake could not be convinced. They unpacked and had time for a swim before dinner. They both swam laps until they were tired, releasing some of their pent up energy. Afterward, they changed and headed for a restaurant in the hotel. The lovely food they ordered sat almost untouched and conversation was light.

At last Jake said, "Sara, I don't know what will happen when and if you see him. I'm as confused as you are, but one thing I do know is that I love you and I love you enough to do whatever you want me to, even if it's to go away."

She looked at him with tears in her eyes. "Jake, please. Let's not talk about it. There will be enough time for that later. Let's just try to enjoy what might be our last dinner together."

Nothing else was said and they both slept fitfully on opposite sides of the bed.

Without an address, finding the man Patsy thought was Peter meant counting on some luck. Patsy had said she had seen him every couple of days – always at the same bar – a creature of habit which was typical for island living. Sitting on their beach chairs trying to enjoy the sun the next day, Sara kept her eyes peeled, hoping – if it was true that he was here – that he had not decided to go on vacation!

She found herself looking everywhere for him. All she wanted to do was to walk and to search. She was torn – almost embarrassed to be with Jake, and that was a horrible feeling. What if Peter saw them first? Saw them together? What would he think? She had to know as quickly as possible if he was alive and if he was here. She wanted the wait to be over.

It tore her heart out to look at Jake because he looked so sad. He was unable to hide his worry and concern, but opposed to her, he did not want to know if Peter was alive. He wanted to hang on to Sara as long as possible. Fear of losing her clearly showed in his eyes. Because she felt sorry for him, she agreed to spend a morning walking on the beach. She promised to forget about it just for one morning, even though she knew it was a lie. She could never forget about it.

The beach walk was invigorating. It was lovely being in the sun and barefoot in the sand. Before they knew it, they were engaged in hunting for shells. Both filled their pockets with colorful shapes and then Sara hit pay dirt when she came upon a beautiful Triton's trumpet about 8" long. She squealed with delight. How rare to find one that wasn't broken! She tipped it this way and that to be sure it was not inhabited. When she showed it to Jake, he impulsively hugged her.

"Hopefully it's an omen," he said, "that this is all going to turn out all right." His smile broke a bit of tension, but all in all there wasn't much conversation going on between them.

Later, back in their villa, she washed the shells and laid them on paper towels to dry. If this was their last day together, at least she would have these beautiful mementoes. She turned to Jake.

"There's one thing we have not discussed and it's hanging in the air between us," she said.

"I know, Sara. You don't even have to talk about it. If you find Peter and you decide you want to be with him, I will immediately leave. Don't worry."

She nodded her head and turned away with tears in her eyes. There would be no good solution to this problem.

The next morning, the vigil began again. It didn't take long before it was fruitful. There he was, before her watchful eyes, walking down the beach with an attractive woman, just like Patsy had said. Sara's heart was in her throat. Her feelings were all jumbled up. Her throat constricted and she couldn't speak. Jealousy reared its ugly head.

She tapped Jake on the arm and pointed. Jake was as shocked as she was. "How can this be?" he murmured. "It sure looks like him. What kind of deception is going on here? No, it can't be him, but it sure looks like him."

"I have to say," he continued. "This strain has been killing me and now I'm feeling mad. I'm feeling like he not only screwed you but he screwed me too. He set us up, Sara. Don't you dare take any of the blame for this!"

"I've been thinking, Jake. I want to approach him by myself and when he's alone too. Let's just get out of here and wait. Plus I want to get a little more used to this idea so I can have my wits totally about me when I finally confront him. If he's here now, we will find him again."

CHAPTER THIRTY ONE

Sara and Jake signed up for an excursion the next day and tried to have fun, but the whole idea of Peter's presence hung over their heads. They were looking for him everywhere they went, but the next day they didn't see him at all. It was another day when they were sitting in a corner on the bar patio having a drink when Sara looked up and said, "There he is."

Jake looked in the direction her head was turned and was glad. This had all been too unnerving and stressful. He said, "OK, let's go. Let's get this over with." He tried to be commanding, but his voice was so nervous that he gave his fear away. Jake was vacillating between running away and running over to punch his old friend.

"No, Jake. He's alone and like I said before, I think I should go alone. If it is him, it has to be between the two of us. What am I saying? Why am I saying IF? We both know it's him. Despite what happened between us, you had and have nothing to do with what happened between Peter and me." She spoke firmly and he knew she meant it. He also knew she was right.

They watched Peter walk over to the bar where he was greeted warmly by the Bartender. He sat down on a stool, ordered a drink and started chatting. Peter motioned to a waiter for their bill and signed it to their room. He said, “I’ll go wait in the room.”

“I’ll come with you just for a minute.”

When they got there, he turned on the news. It made background sound, but he wasn’t hearing a word of what was being said. Instead, he heard Sara go into the bathroom, then the toilet flush, then her puttering around freshening up her make-up.

When she finally came out, she walked straight to him and desperately threw her arms around his neck. He hugged her back and they stood that way for several minutes. He could feel the tension in her body, but neither said one word.

Finally she broke away and looked him in the eye. “Now or never. I have to do it.”

“I know. It’s just that I feel like I want to protect you. I don’t want you to be hurt. And besides, I’d like to give the jerk a piece of my own mind too.”

Her eyes glistened. “Thank you. I understand. But this is first between Peter and me. I’m sorry, Jake.”

“**YOU** have nothing to be sorry for. **YOU** did nothing wrong. Don’t say that. He set you up for everything that has happened. Don’t forget that,

Sara. Don't get all sappy on me and start feeling sorry for him, OK?" He was angry and it showed in the tone of his voice.

"Damn," he said, picking up a sofa pillow and throwing it as hard as he could at the wall.

She was quiet for a moment and then said, "OK."

When Sara turned and walked out the door, his eyes teared up again. He went to the window and watched her walking back toward the bar, not knowing if things could ever be the same between them again and wondering if she would even come back.

CHAPTER THIRTY TWO

Sara walked with resolve. Her eyes were dry and she felt a cold sense of urgency. Fearful and uneasy about what she would find, she distracted herself by counting the steps it took her to reach the bar. One hundred and twenty, one hundred and twenty-one, one hundred and twenty-two. *One foot in front of the other* she told herself. It seemed like it took an eternity for her to arrive.

And then there he was with his back toward her. She stopped and stared at him. She knew that neck, those shoulders, the strong legs and the cowlick in the back of his light brown hair.

The instant she saw him, all the old feelings came rushing back. She suppressed an impulse to run to him and wrap her arms around his neck but was soon thankful she didn't.

Peter was signing his check and then handing it to Henry, the bartender. "See 'ya later, John," he said.

Henry looked up and saw Sara staring at Peter. He laughed and teased, "Hey, it looks like there's a pretty lady there who wants to meet you."

"Alright! Maybe it's my lucky day!" Peter said. He laughed also, stood and turned around. When he saw her, the color drained out of his face.

Her stomach felt like it dropped on the floor. There was something different in his eyes. Something cold. Something pleading. It was an exasperated look. She could see in an instant that he felt like a cornered animal.

He simply said, “Sara”.

“Hi Peter,” she said softly. “Or is it John now?”

“Uh. Both!” he replied, quickly recovering his composure and actually smiling so Henry would not suspect. “Let’s get out of here.”

They walked out to the beach and she sat down on a beach chair. Peter grabbed another one and moved it across from her, facing her but sitting closely together.

He was shocked and confused. She wanted to scream at him. She even considered slapping him. But initially both were speechless. For several minutes, they just sat there and looked at each other, anger and confusion welling up, dying down and welling up again.

He spoke first. “Sara, I’m sorry. I’m so sorry.”

She exploded. “Sorry! Is that all you can say? You’re **SORRY** for lying, cheating, leaving and letting me think you were **DEAD**?” She was stammering. “What about Bogey? He pined for you for a long time.”

“I didn’t think you would ever find out. I thought it would be easier for you if I simply left than if we had to go through a divorce.”

He added, “And I did miss Bogey. I missed you too. But I thought – think – it was for the best. It was best to have no good-byes.”

“Well let me set you straight on that one. It wasn’t. Do you have any idea what I went through? Why, Peter? Why did you do this to me? I thought we loved each other!”

He sat still, looking forlorn. She stared at him in disbelief as he said, “Because it was so easy.”

“What do you mean **SO EASY?”** she cried.

“I was on the steps, leaving for an appointment when the building blew up. I blacked out for a while. I don’t know how long. When I woke up, there were people standing over me asking if I was OK. Some Red Cross person bandaged my arm, told me to see a doctor and was on to the next person. Then I simply walked away.”

He went on. “At first I thought I would walk home or find a cab and then I realized all of my identification was in my office. I was actually headed back to get it when the blast happened. When I thought about that, it seemed meant to be. I mean, I was unidentifiable. I was nobody. I was free. I could walk away and no one would know."

"Ouch," Sara said. "Please tell me you had amnesia?" She looked at him questioningly.

He looked back at her with pity. When she saw that, it hardened her conviction and tore into her soul. "No, Sara," he said simply. "Not at all." There was a pause where he wrung his hands. "Sara... Please try to understand." He reached to take her hands in his. She jerked them away.

"Sara. It's not like I had no regrets. I looked after you."

"What are you talking about?!"

"I had someone watching over you to make sure you were OK. I even had a representative at my funeral." He smiled.

"What the hell? You're crazy. What the hell? She stammered again. Who are you talking about?"

"Giuseppe Balduccio. I call him Joe. We did business together. I had him watch out and make sure you were OK."

"Wait, I saw a big Italian guy hanging around a few times. Is that who you mean?"

“Yes. Must be.”

“Is that how you did it? Did he help you? How did you get away with no money?”

Peter sighed. “Look. Like I said, Joe and I did some business together – actually a lot of business. Some of it might not have been on the up and up and I squirreled away the money in an account. Initially I thought you and I would use it for retirement.”

“I know. You set up an account in Switzerland. And you kept it a secret. You crazy Bastard. “I don’t even know you!” She was stammering again. “How in the hell did you come up with this idea?

“I don’t know,” he said morosely. “It just happened and then the fund got so big. It became enough to start a new life and then when I had the chance I simply took it. After the bombing, I got myself to Joe and he got me here. I made a brand new start. I owe it all to him.”

She looked down at the floor, shaking her head. As she raised her eyes, she noticed his wrist. “Oh my God,” she cried. “You’re wearing your Baum and Mercier! Did you also have him break into my house?”

“Our house,” he said. “My house too and my watch. I wanted it back and I wanted some other things in that box. Some numbers and cards. I had a shallow false bottom put into it to uh… secure some information. And then I needed the information. One of Joe's guys took care of it. What's the big deal? He was careful and nobody got hurt, including Bogey." He smiled. "I told Joe how Bogey is a sucker for a steak."

"Right under my nose," she said. "Peter, how could you?"

"Well, you weren't a very inquisitive type." He laughed.

"Ha ha" she said sarcastically. "Lucky you."

"I **WAS** lucky. We had a lot of good years together. I…"

She cut him off. "Spare me," she said.

There was a pregnant pause where they simply stared at each other.

She spoke first, haltingly. "It means nothing to me now. Nothing at all."

"Sara, have a heart. You know things were not that great between us and they hadn't been for a while when I decided to leave. Frankly I'm surprised that you're this upset."

"There are better ways to handle some situations," she said wryly. "We could have fixed ours."

"Do you really think so? I don't and it was just so easy this way."

"There it is again. So easy. So easy for YOU maybe."

Another few minutes of loaded silence followed.

This time he spoke first and he was such a great actor that he actually seemed sincere. "I'm sorry. I really am."

"Sorry, humph. At the moment I just can't comprehend that."

She went on. "So what now? Now that I know, are you coming home? "

"What is **HOME** anyway?"

"I hate it when you answer a question with a question. I always thought it was a sign of superior intellect, but now I know that it's a sign of deceit. A sign that you don't want to answer my question. So let me answer it for you. We always said it was wherever we were together," she countered. "But it's also where we live – where we built a life together – where we took vows to stay and support each other. Or did you forget about that? I guess twenty five years doesn't mean much to you."

He was silent for a few minutes, staring at her. Then he spoke slowly.

"I guess I didn't realize how long a lifetime could be. It's a long time, Sara. People change."

He looked at her sympathetically. "And don't forget. I am supporting you. I left you plenty of savings and retirement funds and insurance money. So don't give me that. I'm sorry, Sara. I can't do it. I've moved on. I have a wife here." He emphasized the word here.

She looked at him incredulously. "So now you're a Bigamist?"

"I guess so. I mean, now that you know."

"Now that I **KNOW**? Guess what, Peter. You were a Bigamist a long time before that. How can you say these things to me?"

"Sara. That's not all. We have a baby. Angela. She's three months old. I could never leave her."

She was dumbfounded. "Jesus. You've been gone barely long enough for that to happen. You certainly didn't let any grass grow under your feet."

"I can't believe this," she went on. "I know you're younger than I am, but you're still 50 years old. And starting a family? You're crazy."

"Yes, that was part of the reason I didn't return. I wasn't looking for it, but I met Janine right after I got here and we pretty much immediately became involved. When she got pregnant, I knew I would never leave."

"How old is she?"

"She's almost forty, with no other children, so she was ecstatic when she found out a baby was on the way."

"I thought you didn't want any children!"

"I said that because I knew **YOU** didn't want any children. For a long time, I thought I could live with that, but then I realized I couldn't anymore. I had tried to go along with it, but it's part of the reason I walked away."

"Where did you meet her? In a bar the first night you got here? And by the way, why **HERE**? You've never shown a bit of interest in the Bahamas."

"I guess you may as well know. Janine is Joe's sister. When I went to him, he got me a ticket here, arranged for me to get some of my money and sent me to Janine. He said she would take care of me."

"And that she did," Sara said bitterly. "So you didn't just meet her. You were introduced to her."

"Sara," he said disapprovingly. "Try and understand."

There was a long silence. "I'm sorry, Sara."

"Don't say that again, you Asshole. It's too late."

"I know. That's what I'm trying to say."

"One more thing… What about the Insider Trading, Peter?"

"How do you know about that? I mean, what Insider Trading?"

She laughed. "You're going away for a long time, honey."

"Sara, I'm dead, remember? Nobody is coming after me for any Insider trading," he said smugly.

"Yeah. Being dead looks pretty good on you," she threw back.

"They'll never find me," he sneered.

"I can see how you might think that, but I even found you, didn't I?"

"I was wondering about that. How **DID** you find me?"

"I'll never tell. But just don't forget what you always used to say – that it's a small world. It truly is."

She looked into Peter's eyes and didn't recognize what she saw there. The realization that she didn't know him anymore was vivid.

He went on. "Do you want to meet Janine? Do you want to see Angela?" She realized as he spoke that he loved and was proud of his new family.

"No thanks." She sighed. "I'm sorry I didn't know how you felt. I tortured myself because I thought I had failed you, but I realize now that I didn't even know what you wanted – who you were."

She shook her head. "I'm glad we talked because at least now I really understand and I can put this behind me."

She shook her head again, not sure if it was in disbelief or in total realization. "Have your JOE pick up divorce papers next week, OK? I'll have them ready. Then at least you can be legal. **SHE** doesn't even need to know about it. It's my gift to you. Just make sure you talk to her more than you talked to me."

She added, "And after our divorce, don't let me EVER hear from you again."

He grimaced. "Thanks, Sara. I hope you can move on too. I really wish you had somebody too. I think it would help."

"Yes," she said emphatically. That it would. It surely would. Good-bye, Peter." Then she lamely added, "Have a nice life."

They both stood and stared at each other, neither knowing exactly how to completely end it. He leaned over and kissed her on the cheek. She wiped the kiss off with her hand and walked away.

Heading back to the villa, relief washed over Sara's body. Peter was not dead, but he was not what she had thought him to be. He had been "dead" in her mind for so long and now it no longer mattered. She knew she didn't love him anymore. She also knew that he would be found and punished. She felt sure that he would wait there long enough to get the divorce papers and that would be long enough to set his capture in motion. *It would be so easy,* she thought and smiled at the thought.

She rounded the last bend and looked toward the cottage. Jake had left the outside light on and somehow he had found a big yellow ribbon and figured out how to hang it on the door. She grinned, never more sure of where she belonged. The way back to the villa had seemed much shorter and certainly sweeter. Her pace quickened as she headed home.

ABOUT THE AUTHOR

Lynn M. Miller and her husband, Randall

With Zoe and Corrie

Lynn M. Miller is a freelance Journalist. In addition to a rich background in business (including a degree in Business Administration) she is also an accomplished chef. Lynn also holds a degree in Culinary Arts and is the author of the "Flavor Secrets: Back to the Basics" cookbook, which contains recipes, lessons and chef tips for all levels of home cooks.

She is also the author of the first Sara Jensen story, released in July of 2014. Called In Jeopardy!, the novel is available at www.amazon.com as an e-book or paperback. So Easy is the sequel to that novel, but can be read independently on its own and is also available as an e-book or paperback.

Lynn writes a regular culinary column for the Bloomfield Hills Living Magazine as well as many other articles in other genres and a Wordpress Blog at www.cheflynnmiller.wordpress.com. She hosts the Flavor Secrets Cable Television Cooking Show. After shows air, they can be found on her YouTube Channel.

For more information and book reviews, please go to: www.spitzpress.com.

INTERVIEW WITH THE AUTHOR

SPITZ PRESS LLC

Interviewer: *How do you approach writing your books? Is your method structured or unstructured?*

Author: *My first book, "**In Jeopardy**!" absolutely poured out of me. I couldn't have stopped it if I had tried. It was written in 1997, before the extreme mass communication and the writing tools we have today. So whenever I got an idea – which could have been anywhere – I wrote it down on whatever I could find. I was afraid of forgetting, so I had notes on the backs of golf cards, envelopes, scraps of paper or whatever was available. Then I would go home and integrate my ideas into the book on my computer.*

Interviewer: *Did you have a general plan for the book in your head?*

Author: *No, not really. It simply formed itself. I honestly had no idea where it was going!*

Interviewer: *How about **SO EASY**? Did you write it in the same fashion?*

Author: *No, not at all. I knew how I wanted the book to begin and end because of the original idea I had for it. In this case, I wrote the beginning and* *the end first. Then I outlined chapters and went back to complete them. As I wrote, other ideas emerged and other chapters were added.*

Interviewer: *What was that original idea for* ***SO EASY****? Where did it come from?*

Author: *I had the idea for a plot like this almost immediately after 9-11-2001, when the twin towers came down in New York City. I was intrigued by the idea that someone who was thought to have died in there could have used the opportunity to disappear. But that was such a catastrophe. I was afraid people would not be ready to entertain this idea.*

Interviewer: *Are any of your characters real people?*

Author: *Yes and no. I think every author must somewhat base invented personalities on people they have met, whether they realize it or not. I tried not to, although there are a few cases where I consciously did. There are times when it helps in creating dialogue if you base a character on a strong personality type that you know. You can think about what that person would say in a particular situation. It's only a basis for the character though, not an exact replica of that person.*

Interviewer: *Did you use anyone's name that you know in your books?*

Author: *I tried very hard not to! Although in* ***SO EASY****, Marta's name and description are based on one of my former students. I may do that a bit more in the future.*

Interviewer: *You are also an accomplished chef. How about your cookbook? What was the premise of that?*

Author: *I went to culinary school for fun and to throw better parties. There was no thought in my head of getting a job. However, people asked me constantly to teach them what I was learning so I started a class schedule. I taught for seven years and still do an occasional group class. The cookbook was written as lessons for those students. Each chapter of* **FLAVOR SECRETS: BACK TO THE BASICS** *starts out with the most important things to know about the chapter topic and includes recipes that illustrate techniques. It's great for new cooks, but experienced cooks can sit and read it and become better at what they do. One of the reviewers called it two years of cooking school between its covers. That was dead on because my goal was to include everything they teach in school, but in a way that the home cook would feel comfortable trying the techniques.*

All of Lynn M. Miller's books can be found at www.amazon.com and www.spitzpress.com .

Thanks for reading!

*Please **LIKE** and share your thoughts on our Facebook page.*
We would love to hear from you!!

www.facebook.com/spitzpress

BOOK GROUP QUESTIONS

1. How does the Golda Meir quote at the beginning relate to the story? (She said, *"Trust yourself. Create the kind of self that you will be happy to live with all your life."*)

2. The theme "So easy" is throughout the book. What are the different scenarios where it comes up? Is there a better title or is it appropriate?

3. Greg says, "Everyone is responsible for their own greed." Do you agree with that?

4. Put yourself in Sara's shoes. Would you have handled her last conversation with Peter differently?

5. Why do you think Sara fell so immediately for Marta?

6. Do you think Sara did the right thing in leaving the group therapy sessions?

7. Standing in the museum, Sara says she thinks that people should keep their secrets to themselves. She takes no solace in sharing them with a group. Do you agree?

Or do you think she was simply too traumatized to benefit from group therapy?

8. In therapy, Sara *"was suddenly a little curious about where she was in the grieving process but she didn't really care. What difference did it make?"* Do you think it makes a difference to understand and pay attention to the stages everyone goes through? Does it help to know or do you just need to plough through them?

9. Is there a better way that Jake could have handled his involvement with Sara? Do you fault him in any way?

10. How about Patsy? Do you think Sara's forgiveness of her was appropriate? In the same circumstances, could you forgive her for her lack of loyalty, for her jealous accusations of Jen and for her plan to take off with no explanation?

11. If you were Sara and Peter had acted differently and wanted to come home, could you take him back?

ACKNOWLEDGEMENTS

This is the most important part of writing any book.

I cherish the chance to say thank you to those who are always unconditionally by my side.

I am indebted to:

My truly wonderful husband, Randall

My mom, Shirley, and my mom-in-law, Ruth

My Siblings, Mark, Michelle, Barbi, & Tom, who continue to shape my life

My amazing children and grandchild, Aaron, Eric, Christine, and Luke

My friends, Joseph Conceison and Julie Young

My girlfriends that I know I can always call on – who always drop everything

and come running if they are needed:

Alison, Christine, Debbie, Diane, Joy, Karen, Leanette, Mardi, Nancy, Patti, Perry & Talbot

Thank you from the bottom of my heart for your loving support and friendship.

23929959R00125

Made in the USA
Middletown, DE
09 September 2015